Feasting With The Deacon

Copyright © 2006 Leonard Barry Barrington
All rights reserved.
ISBN: 1-4196-2358-3

To order additional copies, please contact us.
BookSurge, LLC
www.booksurge.com
1-866-308-6235
orders@booksurge.com

Feasting With The Deacon

A Novel about the Active Life of Silas benGaddiel

To Richard & Judy with love

Leonard Barry Barrington

Barry B.

2006

Feasting With The Deacon

SALUTATION TO FEASTING WITH THE DEACON

Greetings! I am Silas, ('Silas benGaddiel'), now Serving as Host for this banquet. I shall also accompany You, guiding you on a tour of Macedonia and parts beyond in this, the time of Nero .

Born in the 37th Year of the reign of Gaius Octavius **Augustus**, I am the son of Titus Gaddiel Lucanius, a Roman soldier and scribe who retired to farming in the Jordan Valley. He had earlier married my mother, Miriam, who had inherited the farm on the West Bank where I was born.

I enjoyed the duties of a scribe, and considered following my father's profession, but was also drawn to my mother's kitchen, whereby I learned how to assemble meals from available ingredients.

One day, as I tended our garden, I saw John the Baptist walking with Jesus, apparently just after the great Baptism. Quite a sight! and one that began to frame my dedication to missionary service.

Paul, (once called Saul of Tarsus), was beginning his journeys, and invited me here to Greece and Macedonia. We stopped at Corinth for quite a long time, and the good people there would have named me Overseer/Bishop, but I chose instead to return to Berea, the Macedonian mountain village that had captured my imagination from my first view of it, some five years earlier. I held a vision of small churches —churches I could think of as "Gardens for God". For the people of Berea, I can also present the successes of my cooking in the tasty fare I have developed, thinking of the results as "The Deacon's Sizzlers".

So, I believe I have given enough information on my origins and intentions. Now we should look ahead to **Feasting**. Peace to you all.

I could not have accomplished the deeds of my life without the inspiration and assistance of many, including Madeleine L'Engle (in whose creative writing class at Mundelein College the first chapter of the 'Deacon' saw light), Susan Power, Father Arthur Tonne, John Ferpotto, Emil Dillard, Marsha Portnoy, Guy Houston, Sister Mary Isadora, Reverend Clarence Agard and especially SharynMarie -- my dear and patient wife, my late parents and all my teachers since 1930. They and all my intimately held friends of the past and present deserve much of the credit for my trophies, but none of the possible blame for my missteps or the Deacon's shortcomings.

CHAPTER I.

A.D. 54 —SETTING OUT FOR MACEDONIA

✳✳✳

'Silas leads; Silas feeds.,' So associates of the deacon say in both Antioch and Corinth. At the picnic here in Corinth, Silas the Deacon faces the blazing noon-day sun. Peering down the hillside at the Lechaion Road below the smoky picnic area, he sees a contingent of uniformed soldiers approaching in march formation. With an expression of sudden concern, he tells himself, "That slogan: Today, it might read 'Silas feeds, Silas bleeds'!"

Laughing at his own statement and also at its unlikely fulfillment, he turns to his friend —his fellow missioner —Timothy: "Brother, I hope these soldiers do not officially object to this heavy smoke from the cooking fires."

Timothy speaks reassuringly to him: "After all, Deacon, the Corinthian council gave us a permit to use this place to celebrate your leaving. Actually, I foresee a pleasant encounter with these men." "Perhaps," says Silas. "Maybe I'll just hop down to prepare the pathway for that outcome, or —if necessary —to do bloody battle on the hillside…. I am joking, Timothy."

The hillside is a barren incline —its soil dusty and profuse with paths that missionaries and prostitutes, as well as criminals and soldiers, have formed with their feet. Several of the Roman officers now plant their sandals on one of those paths to climb up toward the sweet and aromatic preparations from Silas's outdoor kitchen, borrowed, as usual, and borrowed today from his friend Junius. "Look!" Silas shouts. "In truth, these appear to be men of a quality to match our treats." He fills a basket with appetizers. Then he scoots, barefoot, down the sun-baked incline toward the Lechaion to meet them…. "Greetings, Brothers," he addresses them in somewhat hesitant Latin. "I meet you here in the blazing Grecian sun to share appetizers from our noon-time picnic. Won't you have some fruits, some cheeses and samples of our freshly baked hard breads? I am preparing a meal —a complete farewell picnic, as I will explain —a meal we wish to share with all of my mission community, as a gift."

The leader of the contingent wears the insignia of a Cornicular. Silas touches his badge in a way that honors it: with the faces of his first two fingernails, right hand. Smiling, he nods to the officer, who personalizes his salute saying, "My men tell me that you are in charge of a new cult here and that you carry loving charity everywhere.... Well?"

Silas replies: "Cornicular, uh, sir, I am honored to lead my small congregations which devote themselves to the Way. I also create a cloud of smoke when I cook. Are we in trouble?"

The Cornicular waves off Silas's query with a proposition: "No, not in trouble unless you try to stop us from sampling the foods you are cooking. Such a fragrance!" he continues, in Greek, *"Eides aromi!* Can you not see tastiness in it? I can. I saw its trail winding, wafting down along the curvature of these heights. That smell is likely to lure every hungry mouth in the city!"   Not waiting for his junior officers, he waves them to climb with him, asking Silas, "Do we know you? I would propose that you, the cook at the top of the hill, should be placed into service in Claudius Caesar's Imperial Army, in the officers' kitchen."

"No, Cornicular, you do not know me, and I have tried to remove myself from direct service to the Emperor by serving his people. I am Silas benGaddiel; some call me the Feeding Deacon: Deacon Silas. And you are—?"

With a broad smile to Silas, the officer announces loudly: "I am Zaccur Tobias Publius, should you wish to know my name. You should remember to salute me as the Cornicular. Close friends call me 'Tobi.'" Pausing at a wayside landing where the troops join him, Silas silently mouths 'Toh—bee' and turns the name into a puzzle about its origins.

Although he postpones consideration of that puzzle to a later time, he listens carefully to his visitor, who continues, "I understand that you are the Silas who carries loving everywhere and who arrived some three years back, joining a man some recall as the Pesky-Preacher Paulus. Is our barracks record correct on that matter?"

"Sir, yes, I have been here for almost three years and arrived with

FEASTING WITH THE DEACON

Timothy, who stands at the hilltop now. As your records also show, we came to join our companion, Paul —you referred to him.... Paul has left and come back and left and come back, and I believe you will discover that he, too, has recently returned to Corinth again. Your characterization, 'pesky': I shall leave that to your discovery, if you will permit me, sir."

"Yes, I, too, shall leave that topic. Can I persuade you to share some of your banquet with my men, Deacon? These soldiers have a notorious reputation for violence if they do not —"

Aware of his sharp teasing, Silas interrupts him: "We do not require a test of their ability to do violence, Officer Tobi, but we have to wait for the meal itself to mature. It is not yet at that point. As the meal progresses, I will prepare a delicious kakavia, which you will not want to miss."

"Really? Kakavia? Yes, I shall want some, and I have a ferocious dread of waiting in the summer sun for the meal to mature. Nevertheless, I shall do so and hope my men will also be welcome."

"Cornicular, how greatly I wish we could accommodate them, but no, since this is a special, special time for us. No, we would not be prepared for so many others at our table. Nonetheless, as a special treat for us, I would be honored to stand behind that cloud of smoke to add more food if you will join us personally."

He stands aside, flashing a broad smile. Silas and the Cornicular beam at one another, slapping palms and then exchanging a rough hug in the Corinthian heat. No air stirs to take away the intensifying cloud of smoke over the cooking fires along the hilltop.

Silas, who would return to stand 'behind that cloud of smoke,' admits, "I am preparing to leave Corinth, where I have led the formation of three missions. Within the creed called **The Word and The Way**, I speak at my missions every week." By paying quiet attention to his words, congregations thereby risk the scorn and possible punishment by Rome.

Silas is quick to explain the risk. "It is not because of what we believe, not because of our special worship form. But —but it is because of what we do not believe, and what we do not do in honor of the gods of Rome —or the gods of Greece, for that matter. We do not —as you well know —we do not offer sacrifices to them to obtain their favor. I often ask, 'And why is that? Does anyone want to tell us? Anyone?' But no one ever offers a reply. 'Very well. Later,' I say, keenly aware of the price these friends might have to pay for their refusal to worship the dozens of Hellenistic divines in their panoply of gods. In fear, instead of love."

3

This meal, this planned picnic is to be the centerpiece of a farewell Silas is preparing in love for his guests. He has cooked much of it, as he says, "to share as a parting gift for the men and women who will be the core of the Corinthian missions, the parokias, when I have departed for Macedonian Berea." He began to explain, "I am preparing a meal, a farewell meal, but one we wish to share as a gift to all of them."

The Cornicular Tobias now tried to interrupt with his own side of the conversation, but Silas the Deacon left no opening —not yet. He continued, "When I go to Berea, to Macedonia, they will be left in charge."

"In charge? In charge of what?" the Cornicular asked with no little exasperation, "You know that the Emperor's forces are in charge of everything in Corinth. You have not learned how to pass the tests which the Emperor's tough officers apply to break the spirits of provincial activists, have you?"

Silas ignored the implied insult and merely smiled in a manner that would usually have won the day. He tried another approach: "We have not yet started to cook the grilled foods or the kakavia stews; they will be on the table somewhat later, Cornicular."

"Oh, these are fine.... Just right, friend! These first appetizers are fine." Zaccur Tobias then said with conviction, "Keep them coming. Eh, men?" And his junior officer staff members all nodded, smiling, adding grunts and the little round of informal applause that makes such encounters pleasant. Continuing in broken Latin, Silas volunteered "Gentlemen, you may wonder that we have chosen this hour, hot under Corinth's fiercely flaming sun, to set our picnic fires. As my friends here know, I am leaving at about dawn tomorrow to go north, and this is our farewell picnic. I have always believed in combining ceremony with the eating of shared foods."

Sensing that it was correct for each party to dismiss the other, Silas then began to climb back up the hill, but the Roman officer raised a hand to hold him, saying, "From what I have heard, Deacon, —you are the local Deacon, I understand? Your friends here will miss you greatly. As far as the Corinthian military post officers have a say in the matter, you may come back to Corinth at any time —that is, any time when you offer such foods as these"; and he roared with laughter at his own attempt at humor.

Silas brightened as they wave a token farewell, adding, "Why not drop back later for kakavia and sweetbreads when you have completed your rounds?"

FEASTING WITH THE DEACON

The officer smiled to his men and smiled even more broadly to Silas, making a slight bow of his head, and, remembering the deacon's earlier comment, asked "Did you really promise kakavia? Genuine kakavia?"

Silas was quick in response: "Yes, Cornicular. Genuine, of course, with squab, scallops, fish, herbs, and wine. We will also tempt you by serving the kakavia on toasted hard bread in soup plates. It is a truly excellent dish. Just ask my friends, who make a habit of destroying it!" And the gathered troops all cheered, shouting out their anticipation with appropriate calls.

"I suspect," Tobi added, "that eating it is a raging habit. I ought to avoid such temptations as your cooking but will keep it in mind all afternoon as we proceed through our round of tasks."

Each of them then sensed that they should go on about their business, and they took their farewells. The soldiers reassembled around the Cornicular, and Silas simply continued his slow climb back to the top of the hill. If puzzles remained, they could be solved later.

When he returned to duties at the grill, Silas addressed his friends. "I arrived early," he said, "to take up the cooking; also to insure that I can greet everyone as they arrive." Several women guests had already touched his sleeve, and Timothy and Junius had shared shoulder hugs with him.

Silas then turned to those gathered —the group would grow to more than 300 persons —and announced his recipes, as had become his custom. "For the easy one," he declared to anyone within earshot, "we are relying on the great eggplant in a Macedonian recipe. As Timothy recalls, I'm sure, it was prepared for him, Paul and myself when we stopped in Berea a few years ago. We do have a good crop of eggplants here."

"You know , the Corinthians call them melitzanes," Timothy reminded, "*Meli*, honoring the touch of honey-sweetness that comes from stewing them."

Silas nodded, agreeing. "I am not always open to your Greek lessons, Timothy," he said. Sometimes they do not teach me what I want to know! What I want to know right now is whether Paul is here. I'd like to count on his memory for the eggplant salad...."

"Junius!" called the barefoot deacon across the top of the tent. The tent was actually shorter than Silas, as his sight-line was also well above the heads of his friends —especially higher than the pleasant, wiry Dorcas who was busy building a fire in the second cooking pit. Dorcas wheeled her short body around to draw Junius away from his conversation with other friends, and she turned him into the line of Silas's sight. Junius shrugged his shoulders to signal that there was no sign of Paul. "No, the great busybody is not hereabouts," he reported.

Dorcas volunteered, "May I help you, Deacon?"

Silas welcomed her help. "You know, in the Jordan Valley, we had but few occasions to cook and enjoy eggplant, but, according to my memory, here's how we prepared an appetizer dish called eggplant salad —*Melitzanosalata*, a cooked salad. With your common sense, Dorcas, maybe we can make an eggplant stew recipe to please our palates. For this, if for nothing else, you shall remember me when I'm in Berea.... Dorcas, please tell Junius that we'll want ripe olives with this, as we proceed with our wine sipping and chat." "Here goes for *Melitzanosalata*: Fires first. Build them to the edge of glowing. With that —we bury two eggplants in a moderately hot bed of coals, as we have here. We'll remove them from the heat at the end of a short hour, allow them to cool, peel them and discard the skin. Chop the warm eggplant into a clay bowl we have rubbed with garlic. Beat the eggplant choppings with a heavy spoon, along with chunks of squash and something my Mother called "red," adding small amounts of ladi oil and vinegar plus pinches of oregano and pepper or other sharp herbs. Beat and mix until you have made a smooth, creamy paste."

While he spoke and described his recipe, Silas also sang scantlings of Galilean children's songs, such as 'Hop around the Rocks', and he joined Dorcas in preparing the dish itself, tasting it from his fingertips when he saw it was complete. Then he said, "There, we have prepared the eggplant salad. Sprinkle it with slices of black ripe olives, and enjoy."

"Oh, my dear Silas," called the lovely Dorcas, "I believe you forgot the salt."

"Of course, you are correct —we cannot really enjoy it unless it is correctly salted!" the Deacon agreed. "I guess I am just tall enough to lift my head up into the land of forgetting. There, that's enough salt; we have made it just right, just as they prepare it in the Jordan Valley. Now, we let it stand in a cool place. Here: *eides aromi!* Again, see that great smell! See **that** smell, will you!"

Those nearest to him sniffed, nodded and smiled —these Corinthians from three neighborhoods, three parokias, who had helped build the city's three meeting houses. Three churches that sang for the three

FEASTING WITH THE DEACON

parokias, praising God and serving the people of the bustling port and trade center. Yesterday, on that huge hill south of Corinth, Silas had led the preparation of a feast, a great feast for the homeless and others much deprived. To that hungry throng whom he had given food and love, he also fed hope. Today, his closest friends needed as much. With his friends, as with strangers, he shared.

For more than a year, since he and Timothy had joined Paul, Silas had headed the mission at Corinth. As Serving Deacon, he put forward some precepts and helped connect goals, duties and people. Several said they wanted him ("**Not** Paul!" they had said) to take charge, as Bishop.

He had not enjoyed the diaconate as much as the post he had freely asked for, ten years ago in Jerusalem, but he had done it well; even Paul on being urged, said so. But, 'Bishop' Silas? "No," he asserted, quite definitely. "This, this is the life for me, and I will surely miss these happy gatherings with friends, sharing our meals and our hopes. Our wills are bound, bonded together, but we don't shackle one another."

"When you have fed Corinthians, body and soul, listen for the call to come to Macedonia." Silas had once so preached, and so fed. Now heeding, he was going on, on and back to Macedonia. There, Silas would tend another garden, would nurse orchards, and would prepare other foods to help feed another flock.

Today, for those closest to him, he enlarged and spread derivatives of yesterday's leftovers. Junius offered the open yard behind his house, near the shops; he had added bait to the invitation by remarking, "Silas promises there will be a small plate of sweets and other good food to share."

Re-warming the meats, adding soured cream to the fruit compote, the deacon stayed always near the table but also kept aware of each guest's arrival. Each friend gave or took a hug; Silas engaged them in little songs. Some could only hum the melodies, often adding their own blendings from their origins in Judea, Rome, or Alexandria. Just as often, they murmured some appreciation of the fragrant vapors that wreathed the hilltop, rising from the outdoor hearths.

A dear friend approached the picnic area. "Is this the house?" Priscilla asked herself. "Halloo, Silas, dear old Blue Eyes! Are you here, Silas, my good friend?" The host looked up and interrupted a song; he saw Priscilla coming around the house. He raced to meet her as she approached carrying a covered platter. "What, I wonder, has Prisca brought us?" he inquired, almost informing them all that he knew. But he lifted the cloth, discovering freshly made cheese breads still warm from her oven next door.

"Oh, I know what to do with these!" Silas cheered, giving Priscilla a hug which she returned, adding a kiss.

Preparing to take the next step for the spectacle of feasting, Silas added some more wood to his cooking fires. A cloud of smoke rose over the tent, and Silas wiped the sharp sting from his eyes. Then he reached for a small flask; he drew a modest volume from it, pouring the liquid into the platter of cheese breads.

With a proper flourish, he cleared his throat and raised his voice to catch and hold the group's attention. With a broad smile, he announced, "Cla-a-sss! Stu-u-dents! Co-o-ri-inn-thi-ians! Behold this spectacle! Food and illumination, all in one. Now, watch!" Silas inclined the platter toward his cooking fire to ignite it.

Booooom! The zone around Silas flashed. The platter of special breads exploded, then fell in flames to the earth; then continued to burn as smoke billowed. The cheese breads lay ruined.

Uneasy laughter. Silence. Small sounds. Small laughter. Picking up his scorched hat —the shallow-crowned petasos he wore —Silas spoke again: "Well, this proves a point we have taught earlier in the churches: 'Spirituous liquors can be unsteady servants!'"

"I do regret that this fierce combustion has deprived you of Sister Prisca's tasty breads. Prisca, please accept my apologies; also, I need you to minister to my wounded pride, deeply wounded." Silas poked at his ribs and grimaced, mocking himself, and then chuckled.

Joining the others in their relaxed laughter, Priscilla smiled. "I enjoy a picnic," she said, "where, for once, I am not the one who has to plan or present the entertainment. However, you will have to believe me, Brother Silas: those were the best cheese breads in Corinth!"

The laughter subsided. Everyone made certain Silas was not burned. Some guests began to sample the appetizers and delicacies —olives, cut vegetables, hard cheeses, raisins and almonds and dates. "Phoebe, someone here, maybe you or Aquila, should have a bird stew ready for emergencies such as this…. Ahh —do we have a group of doves ready to stew?"

"Yes, Silas," called Aquila, "I brought a crate of them up here when Prisca and I came this morning, just in case! And I also have a recipe that can put a large bowl of wild dove stew on the table in an hour. It has come down from my friends' ancestors, back twenty generations to Babylon of old, a genuine **Kakavia**:. "You will want to save this". Aquila emphasized. "As you know, Silas, it is called *kakavia*, a simple wild-dove stew based on young doves:Clean the doves correctly, but leave them whole, and then place them in an open pot of water, on heat.Make a rubbing of mint and salt and apply to the insides and outsides of the doves, which are then replaced in water along with an addition of some vinegar. Heat in slowly boiling water until doves are tender for serving. Drain them and present for dishing out. Enjoy!

"Should I write those directions for the first step? No?" Aquila continued, "Well, you probably already knew the way to stew doves, but we needed time to recover from Silas's unholy blast, and we do require a main dish, the other having gone with the wind, as it were."

Then Aquila began to laugh and Silas joined him, laughing at himself: a great roaring laugh. Then he stopped the laughter, his hand in the air. He called out, "We need to add seafood to this to make a first-class kakavia dish, a true kakavia with all the richness we can instill into a meal. Would you please bring in the fish, the bass as well as the shellfish scallops, Prisca? Ahh, thank you. Now, we will have a really tasty meal, I know. I see that we have a marvelous mix of herbs and vegetables to add, and a plentiful variety of wines. While the *kakavia* simmers, I shall relax and visit again."

Shortly after he had taken a seat in a cool spot, Prisca's daughter slipped close to Silas, offering him a bouquet of small yellow blossoms. "Aha!" He remarked, "This young woman offers the barefoot deacon a remedy, a trophy of flowers, a true balm! Thank you; I assume it is freely given."

"Well, not entirely," the young lady slyly interposed. "I will ask you to pay for this bouquet with a song. Please sing 'Flower on the Mountain.'"

"A song later; yes, you shall have that sweet song, even if we have to recruit other singers."

During the pause, Junius stepped up, inquiring in Silas's ear, "Does that comment about strong spirits have a deeper meaning?" And Silas turned quickly and smiled, asking,"Does Jerusalem lie to the East? Yes, friend, it has a deep meaning, and I look to return to that subject."

Resuming his cooking, Silas reported that the eggplant stew had simmered long enough, and he accordingly relocated the stew pot to a place on the serving table. Then he raised his calloused hands, beckoning any and all to thanksgiving and sharing the stew. Timothy arrived just then, exchanged a brotherly embrace, and nodded toward the two bottles of Maronean wine he had brought. He raised the question that everyone always asks of good cooks: "Do you add the wine to the meat in the pot or at the time you start to serve it? And what is your secret for excellent cooked fare?"

Junius interrupted, "I'll take that question. Just as the gods and goddesses of old mixed nectar with water, we should mingle waters and juices with wines. Neither one should overpower the other. Right, Deacon?"

"Yes, Junius, let them mingle," replied Silas. "I don't believe that was Timothy's question, however; I'm thinking he wants to know when to add the wine to the meat. Well, on that, you may let the meat sit in wine for some time before cooking, or while cooking, but after the meat has found its own character.

"Let me add that you have a right to your own method and your own taste. I call that little idea a 'raisin of truth,'" Silas said.

Junius's wife had overheard Silas and asked, "Does tolerance for many tastes lead to debates over choices?" Silas leaned back, smiling, to direct a blue-eyed glance squarely into her face. "Oh yes, lively debates. We should allow them; even more, we should encourage them."

A new sound, a new silence combined then to tell Silas that something or someone had brought change to the attention of the group, and he looked up to identify the cause of it. He peeked through the burn-hole in his ragged, scorched hat brim. He saw a familiar garment, observed a familiar gait, and caught sight of a familiar shaggy beard and balding head. Then he observed the deep eyes, the sparkling grey eyes of the Cilician apostle, which Paul used to help kindle spiritual fires.

To the new arrival, he exclaimed, "Why, Paul! Paul, welcome, brother!" Then he turned to those gathered near, calling, "Friends, Paul, the tentmaker from Tarsus, has joined us. We welcome him warmly."

Pleasant sounds and welcoming words followed, and Paul smiled to acknowledge them.

"Joy to you, Silas, and *shalom*...'*ireni*...' 'Peace.' I come to break bread with my friends. Not being wealthy, I bring little more than my appetites," Paul announced somewhat wearily.

"Welcome, with pleasure, to you and your appetites," said Silas.

"I appreciate your courtesies, Silas, and I know you are attending to a large meal on an occasion. Your heart probably already has a mix of burdens, ahh —"

"—and I hear it coming, Paul, you are about to say 'but,' so I will pause to ask Dorcas to count the dinnerware pieces while we listen to the turn of your words." Silas said. "Who, what, this time, is troubling you, Paul?"

"Some of your flock here, Silas, some who made promises only last month! during my campaign ——they have begun to break certain vows," Paul muttered, worrying the words as he spoke.

"Where, then, may I begin?" Silas asked. "Should I ask you first why you are so disappointed or how you learned of their supposed misbehavior?"

"Surely, you know why their failure disappoints. As for 'how,' I know. Do not forget that some 15 years ago I was a spy for the organized opposition. I have mended my aims, thank God, but I have not 'forgotten the techniques," Paul replied.

"So we see", Silas said. "But Paul, we must let others travel their own roads, make their own mistakes. We help them shape their belief, which does not call for us to police their conduct."

Paul sighed, "Just as I worried: You and I have not set the same standards of performance, and ——oh, I see I am delaying the farewell niceties."

"Yes, brother, you do not see nor set standards and codes of conduct for these our creedal companions, and you are also quite correct in saying that this celebration has been delayed, leaving friends standing in the sun. I have drawn Timothy's red wine for Junius, Prisca and others. Will you also have a glass?"

"Thank you, Silas, but I may have wine later. Just now, I want to clear my thoughts among those friends in the shade of that young olive tree."

As the groups sorted themselves out and re-assembled, Timothy moved near Silas again, inquiring, "You are traveling to Berea alone?"

"Traveling alone, no. Travel will be in part with the Corinthian Cornicular, our newly met companion, and also with Phoebe's nephew. He has agreed to meet us in Marathon; we are planning to go by boat together to a landing quite near Berea and—"

"No, Silas, I mean do you intend to work alone, without Paul or me or other members of the group here? Several of us may be useful for that duty, I am certain."

"Yes, Timothy, I agree, but I shall begin in Berea with just God and me, trying to help that community and to become more God-like myself."

Silas added his continuing concern for Corinth, saying, "I will remember that you also have work to do here, as I have not resolved all local disputes nor melted all the Corinthian quarrels. This flock will require a lot of your prayerful care and illumination, much more than merely arranging meetings."

"I know that, Silas!" Timothy growled. Silas pressed on, with a note of deep caring, "Corinthians still inhabit a spiritual nursery, Timothy. For their sake, you will want to do more than merely stand guard against mockings. Yes, you did hold off those hateful, hating haters recently on your trip to Thessalonica. Thus, all of us older brothers and sisters must continue to help Corinth nourish its community of faithful. I hope that with your continuing counsel they come to glow as lamps, making a brightness that I will be able to see all the way to Berea!"

"I shall try to assure that, Silas but am not totally confident that I can. After all, several things have taken away our strengths: outstandingly, your departure for Berea. Gaius has already gone to Thessalonica; Paul is going to Ephesus or Rome or somewhere else distant. Yes, I have agreed to take it on, here in Corinth, but have I prepared for the responsibilities, Silas?"

"Of course not, Timothy," Silas said. Then, with a twinkle of mischief in his eyes, Silas teased him lightly: "But did you prepare for your responsibilities for this picnic?"

"My —My responsibilities? For the p-p-picnic?" asked the shy missioner, to be met with a roar of laughter from Silas who announced, "Friends, Timothy and I are singing a duet! Come along, Timothy, and join me in 'Flower on the Mountain.' And Timothy gulped and cleared his voice for a Sing-along swatchling of the pretty country song:

Flower on the mountain,Struggling through the snow;Other flowers cannot grow So high up on the mountainside That you decorate with pride; Pretty yellow, pretty yellow flower.Pretti-litti-yetti-litti-pretti-yellow flower.

Prisca's daughter was also pleased by their attempt at yodeling. The other adults cheered; Silas blushed.

FEASTING WITH THE DEACON

Hardly had they finished their duet than Silas saw the Roman officer re-climbing the hill, alone this time. Silas moved slightly down from the hilltop to welcome him: "All right, and welcome again, Zaccur Tobias Publius. You must be quite the social fellow to dismiss your men so quickly and get back to the picnic."

"I knew you would welcome me, and there are a few things I'd like to discuss with you, so I do hope to have an enjoyable hour or so with you and your many friends, Silas Deacon."

On hearing his comments, Silas hurried ahead and called several of his associates to come meet the Roman officer, the Cornicular who sharply insisted on being called 'Tobi.' He was warmly welcomed and showed his appreciation by pulling a small jug of Nemean wine from his loose outer coat. Paul took the jug with admiring relish, and the group completed getting acquainted with Tobi, who set his uniform aside with some weariness. "Go on with the discussion that I interrupted," Tobi said.

Timothy and Paul looked up smartly. "Did our duet sound like a discussion to you?" asked Timothy, who acknowledged Tobi's courtesy and went back to the debates with his missionary colleagues.

"Silas, let me come back to my concern for your situation in Berea," Timothy said. "Do you really know any of the Bereans? Where will you stay? There is only one inn in the village, as I recall, and the host did not make us welcome."

"Well, Timothy, I expect to find Gaius again, and —you remember that man Caleb? The Alexandrian who brought us food during our first sojourn in Berea? Caleb offered his house any time we might need a place," Silas reminded him. "You don't recall?"

Timothy showed an uneasiness. "I guess I had been paying attention to other matters in Berea, Silas. Paul mentioned a man who grumbled about feeding us, grumbled that we were non-productive people of the new faith, and seemed quite uncouth."

"That's Caleb!" Silas admitted. "He is a fitting challenge, but I do not see harm from him. I expect to grow close to him."

"Well, if you recall him in such a special way and look to feel at peace in his home, I hope you are correct in that. I have nothing more to say except that Corinth's considerable loss in your leaving will become Berea's gain on your arriving there. I hope we have time for a word of good-bye and exchange of blessings before you leave."

"Yes, Timothy, we must try to find an opportunity to speak again before tomorrow's dawn, when I shall leave. But I notice that Paul stands yonder. Paul and I must reach agreement on some matters in the philosophical goat chase. Thank you for your good wishes." So Timothy returned to the food and his other friends. Silas now moved over to speak again to Paul, who had the Roman Cornicular Tobias in tow. Silas asked, "Paul, what fault do you find here? Remember, you have worked in Corinth, too; this flock has looked to you also for guidance."

"Silas, these sheep have become your sheep. I was just telling the Cornicular that they seem too much at ease. They do not display the correctness of habit I required of them when I instructed them last year. I warned you that they would stray, and I wonder: Haven't they?"

"No, Paul. Not on my tally card. I offer them the Word gently, and they feed independently, in quiet confidence. How do you find that incorrect or improper?"

Paul replied, "You act as though our preaching makes a pasture where you let them roam freely, grazing here a little and there a little."

"My approach is to make our teaching a form of nourishment, yes, a pasture, if you will. They are not rejecting commandments, Paul. I have taught them how to select the greater good and how to reject and spit out sticks and tricks. They keep the law of love. Paul, I regard love as the most royal of verbs," Silas reasoned.

He continued, "They, too, have come to accept loving as the most noble act, while I think that you regard it as a noun, the subject (or perhaps the object) of a sentence. Do you not also sense that our Corinthian friends are moving toward true happiness as they go about, grazing and nibbling on the parables and the lessons we borrowed from the instructions of our parents and rabbis?"

Tobias, the Cornicular and Chief of Patrol, interrupted: "Excuse me, but what instructions would those be?"

Silas replied, "Ahh, Tobi, perhaps you will recall them from your own boyhood at the synagogue, before the temple. Perhaps, like me, you discovered the legendary <u>Three Things we are to learn from a Child;</u>

Recall: First, always be happy;

Second, never sit idle;

Lastly, when you hunger for understanding,

let your want `be known.

"Remember, Tobi?"

"Yes," said Tobias, "and will that not set you more securely on your way to Macedonia?"

Silas took Tobi's sleeve between his thumb and finger and pulled as he said, "Let me say that I hope my call to Macedonian Berea permits me to enjoy both small and large fruits from my spiritual garden there, sharing them all with the nibblers in that region, even the adjunct nibblers, such as you, Tobi."

Paul fumed, "Silas, this is not the way we are to spread the Message. There is a right way; stand close to that path, or risk great loss!"

"I know you disagree, Paul; we have spoken of this before. As I see it, your way would direct us to destroy the old forest with its mixed beauty, burning it down. You seem to want to replace anything that is already growing, such as apple trees, to replace them with a stand of olives selected for their uniformity and their suitability for commerce. I instead call for planting melon seeds here, where we know melons grow. I will simply continue to try to enrich the soil."

"Stop using phrases drawn from your view of nature! You remind me of the poets of David's time, looking for dawn, for deer, for rain and for love in a bushel of wheat! If you could stick to correct ways and words with strict meanings, we could get a little closer to the harmony I desire in our outlook about the conduct of God's work."

Silas observed smartly, "If you could change, just a little, Saul —I mean Paul —we would make some progress there. God's work will be done, regardless."

"Am I going to have to arrest one of you to get a grasp on the teachings of your Redeemer?" asked Tobias. "I lean strongly toward Silas's outlook and propose to accompany him all the way, with your permission, Deacon. However, I fear I would want little to do with your view of God, Paul."

"Oh, go on, both of you! Get along to Berea, Silas! Your approach, I regret, falls quite outside the narrow path I will require in Ephesus and Rome. Tobias, I realize a sturdy goodness thrives inside Silas's hairy chest, and a great love for people flourishes behind his soft blue eyes. But take note that I am warning both of you: I shall persist in every way available to set you more firmly into the path and on the Way."

"And I shall hope you relax your requirements, Paul," said Silas. "I am going to encourage Bereans to express praise freely and to support one another lovingly, without rock-hard rules —with only a desire to do good and love one another. That, I pray, will encourage many in Macedonian parokias to find joy and give glory. I call that the way to the Way."

He had flavored his voice for oratory, quite unintended. Now that he realized its distancing effect, and seeing the approach of dusk as a basis for escape, Silas dropped to a more sharing tone: "I must go now; I have promised to speak with Phoebe on a matter. Paul, I am not the only one concerned about your inclination toward a church of power, rules and rigid dogma."

"Concerned? What alternative would you —?"

"Alternative? Alternatives, Paul! A free form of worship; an unending search for truth. Unending love." Leaning close, Silas invited Paul to take his hand, "Peace, now. Find me in Berea, Paul." But the man from Tarsus hesitated, permitting attention to be drawn to an interrupting hand on Silas's shoulder. It was Tobi's hand, showing Silas's new connection to the Roman military: Zaccur Tobias Publius. Tobi stepped forward from the gathered group and interposed himself between the two debaters, saying, "I must be going back to the barracks now, but propose to join you in the morning, Silas, and all the way to Marathon."

Both Paul and Silas looked up quickly, Silas saying, "Tobi, your generosity overwhelms me. Are you free to set your duties aside?"

"I have some free time and am expected to survey the lands and minds of every locale. Traveling with you and your small retinue will afford me that opportunity, Silas, and I also have personal reasons, questions that I want to lay before you. Three to five days will give us just sufficient time for them, I believe, if you are willing to pay that price for a Roman military escort."

"I accept, most gladly," said the deacon, "and will look for a great discussion of —

"Watch out!" Paul snapped. "This man is an unbeliever, Silas. He is not offering to accompany you out of charity."

"Whaa-aa-at?" Silas and the Cornicular snorted in unison. "Is that remark to be taken in jest or as a challenge?" asked Silas.

Paul made a wry face and slowly withdrew, moving his hand to his straggly beard. Abruptly, he struck at Silas' shoulder with a blow that mocked and missed. Then he walked away to mingle with those who shared in the fortifications of Timothy's dark red Nemean wine, which the local people called 'lion's blood.'

Phoebe had observed Paul's departure from Silas' side and perkily stepped up to join the man who had truly built the spirit of the Corinthian mission. "I dread your leaving, dear friend," she told him, "and I'm unsure about our members.... Have they seasoned sufficiently? I wonder, do they understand how to love one another joyfully and responsibly?"

Silas wondered if even he could claim to answer that call. He dreaded telling Phoebe how heavily he counted on her continued leadership, a task which meant a rather lengthy hike for her, from Cenchrae to Corinth. It would likely also require her to assert her right and duty 'as a woman' to call for uplifting songs, tolerance, and unselfish accommodation. He knew and he admired her reflection on his support: 'Silas looks at himself and Paul and he often remarks, don't worry about a little wobble,' she was fond of saying; he knew that.

Now, she and Silas were standing together on the hillside where he had been chatting with Timothy and Paul. Phoebe spoke first. "I want to talk to you about the assistance you will enjoy on the journey to Berea, as well as another matter, Silas."

"Another matter?" he inquired, finally removing the burned and tattered petasos; with no hat to restrain it, his wavy hair dropped across his eyes and surrounded his face.

She drew very close, asking his eyes, "Yes, Silas: Martha.... Have you any word, recent word, from Martha of Bethany? As I recall, when you first arrived in Corinth, you told me of a strong bond between you and her, and —"

Silas nodded. "Let me speak plainly on that matter, Phoebe. Martha and I had been good friends, yes, and often taught one another tricks and techniques in cooking. Our friendship could have ripened, might have blossomed in marriage. Since it did not, I can say we both felt a deeper obligation to James and to the congregation in Jerusalem than to our own needs for intimacy. James needs Martha, and —doubling that need, she, too, needs James."

"Oh?" inquired Phoebe.

"Yes, sister. In a message she sent last year, she told me that they plan to marry to better their joint oversight of the Jerusalem congregation. Next question."

"No, no more questions, Silas. We should now be certain about your plans for joining your carriers at Marathon to get underway to Berea. At Marathon, you will be staying with my nephew —you met him here, remember? Adrianos. Then, two days from tomorrow's dawn, you will depart by boat from the seaside below the Marathon plains. Two men, freedmen helpers from Aquila's household, will accompany you."

"Will they help to bring my goods, especially my scrolls?" Silas asked.

"Yes, to Marathon." she replied. "As I understand the plan, they will also help you and my Adrianos on the boat trip to Pydna, then overland to Berea."

"That is about the way Aquila and I outlined it at his house. It appears you have, as usual, taken care of all the important details. I am most grateful to you, Phoebe."

"Silas, you will always be in the hearts of your friends —hundreds —in the Corinthian parokias. At my age, I do not expect to see you again, but your boyish smile will not fade from our memories, and your strong faith will keep us moving toward ways of peace."

"Give me your hand, Phoebe," Silas invited, placing her palm over his heart. "Now, peace be with you." He placed the tattered petasos back on his head and strode toward the house of Prisca and Aquila, where he would sleep during his last night in Corinth.

Awake at dawn, he and the small group of other travelers started for Athens and Marathon to embark for Berea, the Macedonian village that called out to him. In Berea he would weld new and loving connections to God by touching the lives of other men and women —leaders of that region. "Let us gather here at Prisca's kitchen in the early morning," Silas suggested, "and Aquila or I will cook oaten pottage to gladden our bellies before we complete our packing for Berea."

Zaccur Tobias agreed to that proposal. Accordingly, he and Silas slept until the earliest color of dawn in Corinth, when they prepared their food and other materials that should be loaded on the pack animal and then began the long overland trek to Marathon by way of the hills around Athens. They were off!

Berea, here comes Silas! And the Cornicular Searches for Answers on the Road to Marathon:

FEASTING WITH THE DEACON

Zaccur Tobias began his inquiry almost at once. "Is it true that you have superstitions about the return of your Holy Leader ,a second coming in full flesh and bones, and that you hold to similar beliefs about your own life after death?"

"I do not hold to superstitions at all, Tobi, yet I know what you are leading to. What I deeply believe about the resurrection is derived from sightings, actual visitations after our Master was put to death. We do not emphasize flesh and bones; we are not pushing for belief in the power of relics, nor times nor places of past action. We do not carry bones around to prepare for theatrics or magic," Deacon Silas replies.

"How can I come to believe?" the Cornicular presses on, commenting, "So much of this is contrary to my Jewish learning except that this was the mark of the expected Messiah."

"I tell you, we definitely have the Messiah, Tobi. We believers, who saw the evidence in Him, empty ourselves of normal desires and yield all to Him. My burden will be to illustrate that belief and make it so concrete that those who never will have first-hand knowledge of it, such as you —you, too, will come to believe."

Tobi grunted, as in doubt, asking, "How might this figure, Jesus — this Master of your cult —be different from Elijah? How different from some hero who went to Paradise on a chariot of the Sun, or how different from some of the mysteries that arose just next door, as the false worshiping at Eleusis, or the imported goddesses, known false, such as Cybelene resurrections or Isis? How do you answer? As for me, I have no need of them to replace Yahweh, just as I do not accept Jupiter Dolichenus nor unite with those who deify Caesar or worship the vanished spirit of Augustus. How about you?"

Silas took a while to answer. "Zaccur Tobi," he said when he finally began his reply, "our God is your God. God is pure spirit, pure act. God is love, purest love of our fellow creatures for all creeds and ceremonies, although some may not know this Truth, this Emet, this Veritas, Aletheia.... We will likely come back to this discussion, as we proceed.

"At this time, let's just prompt the borrowed donkey to get going. We want to propel ourselves along the roadways to make timely arrival and departure at the Marathon plains."

"Quite right, Deacon, I do not mean to delay us in our missions," said Tobi, giving the donkey a sharp slap above its left flank, all trotting along, as they departed from Corinth.

LEONARD BARRY BARRINGTON
\"I hold You in my meditations, joined by all who approach a new childhood with me."
—Epistle of Silas/

CHAPTER 2

TO BEREA VIA MARATHON, TO BEGIN ANEW

✳✳✳

Dawn. Marathon. Silas, wakening, ruminates on the previous three days; he dedicates the day, offering thanks and praise; he scans the land. Zaccur Tobias stirs....

Last night, they slept without shelter. Adrianos, whose home his Aunt Phoebe had offered, was away from Marathon. According to neighbors, he had 'left for Thessalonica, but will watch for the deacon's party at Pydna.' Silas wondered 'Where, then, is Archos, whom Aquila had charged to continue accompanying our party?' After a brief wait, at a misty distance he saw Archos carrying a filled goatskin and a basket. "Ahh, there is my guide, and it appears that he has a nice load of food for us, Tobi!"

"Yes, Silas it pulls heavily on his arm. Here, Archos, let me —Tobi —take some of that load. You don't know me, but I believe.... "

"Yes, we have met before, Tobi, thank you."

"Here's my hand, Archos, and where did you get that armful?" Silas inquired as a way of greeting. "Such a lovely collection of fruits!"

"A generous household sold these to me for a modest sum when I told them we are from Corinth. His wife has heard of you and Paul, as well as your work. She sent her good wishes, Silas, along with some caution about the storms that have stirred up the open waters to the north."

"Well, I am certainly grateful for that bounty of fruit and for whatever is in the basket. As for their advice about the weather," Silas inserted, "when we locate our captain, I want to try to convince him to take the inland channel in case he had planned to go by way of the open waters. Just now, you and I should look in that goatskin and work its contents into a morning meal."

"Oh, I know what they gave me," Archos announced. "We have these fresh citrus and grapes, as well as this bowlful of creamed curdy cheese." Then he placed all of his gatherings in front of Silas and the Cornicular.

"This will be simple today," Silas observed; "we will merely spread these as companions for the breads baked for the picnic three days ago." He opened a large tablecloth and arranged the foods there, on the hillside where they had slept. "We can eat rather quickly now, and I can look around the Marathon plain before we take off for the little fishing village where Phoebe's nephew lives."

Completing breakfast, Silas walked briskly to the plain below to view it and ponder its role as a battlefield where ten thousand determined patriots, greatly outnumbered, had won against Persian invaders some 500 years earlier. Would future peoples honor Marathon's heroes by memorials or by trying to outdo them? Did Alexander come by here, dream and ruminate? Did Claudius Caesar look on old battlefields such as this as reminders to strive for peace or as practice grounds for further conquests? Had Silas himself not come awake suddenly on hearing, in his dreams, the clash of arms and the cries of the dying? What if.... Why?

This barren strand, he knew, had not gained renown as an inspiration for poets; rather it had spawned people of action, mariners avoiding or facing the threats of narrows, wild seas, marauding thieves and scum of diverse sorts. With his habit of looking for ways to improve outcomes through simple steps, Silas pondered the good effects of food that might have been brought to this plain. What would have been the outcome if the Athenians had offered food to the Persians or if the Persians had brought out picnic tablecloths and spread them on the strand, covered with the bounty of their provisions and offered to the Athenians...? No spears, no swords, but earnest, honest sharing, joining appetites for accommodation and peace , instead of conquest and territory. A dream ahead matched against a view of lost opportunities, repeated through the years; the only change, the changing names of those who died by violence here.

Silas knew the food that might nurture peace; he would prepare meals of such food. To himself, Silas admitted he had been correct earlier: They must link up with their boatman and be on their way, in accord with the boatman's knowledge of the waters through those strange channels. He looked up to see a huge man lumbering toward him; he smiled and tilted his petasos back from his forehead as the giant boomed, "I presume you are the gospel monger Phoebe warned me about!" In a roar of laughter, he continued, "Are you Silas?"

"I am, if you are Adrianos; are you?" Silas asked, unable to recall how Phoebe described her nephew. Adrianos would simply be there. Was this man the designated guide?

"That runt —me? Look at me, I am a Macedonian! I am named Lysimachus, more than once called 'the Shield of Edhessa.' I am not a peacemaker, but a protector of good households. I know you were expecting my neighbor, Adrianos, but he has gone on to Thessalonica and will meet us at the shore station where we come aground for Berea. He tells me you want to help make life happier around those parts, true?"

"All very true, Lysimachus, and I suspect we ought to prepare to get on our way if you and your boat are ready." Seeing the gruff beard nod, Silas turned to his travel companions. "Come along with those leftover foods and bags; we are off to Macedonia."

Tobi helped to load the sailing vessel and joined in their fun of preparation. "You, sir Cornicular," growled Lysimachus, "You are a regular partner of Silas. What do you owe him, Tobi, that you should take time to help so much?"

"I sense a brotherhood, a kinship with him, and I want to support his work to the extent that he is not unfairly treated —not singled out for punishment merely because of his belief. Besides, he is a most excellent artisan in the kitchen, where my appetite is anticipated. So I help him as a person, not as an officer of the Emperor; that's the only answer I can offer you, that I do not owe him anything else."

Lysimachus nodded and grasped his hand momentarily, as if offering strong endorsement of the determination of Zaccur Tobias. He was not alone, of course. The group worked together then and went about the task of throwing off ropes. They got well acquainted as they headed north toward and through the narrows at Khalkis, long famous for its high quality bronze.

There, too, Lysimachus impressed the others with his ability to sail into the breeze —even Archos remarked, "He masters the wind and the fierce tides here! I am a fair captain myself, but his skill leaves me ready to do his bidding. I have not seen his equal in all my days as a ship's helper around the ports near Corinth. Lysimachus, what else can you do so well?"

"Whatever I set out to do!" the giant shouted, laughing.

"So it seems!" Silas agreed. "I hope all of us take on that spirit. We are fortunate to have you as our captain, right?" Yes, right, it seemed, as they took their places on the boat.

Captain Lysimachus found tasks to fit each of his passenger/helpers, all of whom assisted in bringing the boat up the passage and around the horn of Eubea. There followed two days of terrible shore storms, followed by two days that were enjoyably clear. Silas said that he remembered the trip as 'altogether, a grueling run into the warm waters that set the margin of Greece and its northern mountains.' Tobi agreed, also taking note that they had explored the nature of Silas's creeds and convictions.

Giving further emphasis to his assertion, Tobi said, "When he told me that the Followers practice a gentle respect for others, human and all other life, I embraced that Way. And when he told me that you try to avoid harming others, repenting when you do, I decided that it fits my own outlook on life. When he then added that the Way is a path to the paradise of the soul through continuous prayer and praise in the Name of the Master, I knew I should stick with it."

Archos interjected, "I had earlier heard that some Followers believe that they do not need to avoid doing wrong after they have accepted the terms of the Way, which they may do whatever they wish and will still go to Paradise. I am astonished by that claim!"

"So am I, Archos," replied Silas, "and I foresee a serious debate on that point. For me, I do not find that the Master excused any future backsliding as a spiritual reward for piety and devotion. I do not hold that God gives prizes or deferrals on the basis of your relative completeness in traveling the Way, or how nearly perfect the convert has become. In fact, at the time of His own service on earth, the Master made me understand that we are to improve in our path toward perfection by each day's acts and meditations. Those of you who have read my sketchy epistle will have found some of that thinking. For those who have missed that work of writing, I have brought a copy of the scroll for future reading, for reference, and to make it somewhat more perfect. May it and this journey help to lead our souls to Paradise!"

Archos noticed the effort of Lysimachus in bringing the vessel to a landing. "I sense that we have reached Pydna, the closest approach to Berea; correct?" he said, adding, "We have completed this journey, unless Lysimachus disputes me."

"Tie it up!" Lysimachus shouted. It was dusk on the fourth day of sailing; four tired men jumped from the grounded boat and tied it to the piling they found near the shore station. The five men took snacks from the small remains of foods that had been gathered in Corinth, Athens, and Marathon during the past week, anticipating tonight's appetites. Each of them also sampled the red wine Lysimachus had stored safely aboard the boat. As all of them began to give way to fatigue on bedding brought ashore, Silas led them in a recital of glorification. He fell asleep whispering prayers for the journeys ahead and private petitions for peace.

PLODDING THROUGH MOUNTAIN PASSES

After days of tossing on violent waves that threatened the overloaded boat, the entire crew collapsed in exhaustion on the warm beach near the old port of Pydna. Here, the Macedonian Empire had expired some 200 years earlier; here the Romans buried the dreams of Philip and Alexander; here new hopes, built on a strong new faith, could germinate and flower for future peoples of Greece and Asia.

As a blurry dawn pushed through the shore fog, the travelers awoke with painfully stiff muscles, a depleted food pantry, and other problems: Where were they? How far, how long was the road still ahead to reach Berea? Silas came alert and prayed briefly. The crew said he always seemed to be in a quiet prayer! "Give me vision," he asked, also requesting a detailed view of his future and the future of Macedonia.

The panorama he hoped to examine did not unfold. Instead, a door marked 'Hidden Things' appeared before him as in a vision. Was the future of Macedonia as clouded for mankind as the future of his own life seemed to him? Quite possibly. Yet some had called him a Prophet! In simple faith, he turned his face upward, praising the names of the Almighty God, as spoken from Cathay to the Western Sea: 'Absolute, Compassionate, Eternal Great Spirit.' Then Silas stood.

"Let's find Adrianos and start our march to Berea," he called. Silas and the two from Aquila's household picked up their bags and all that they had carried from Corinth through Athens to these harbor shacks. Lysimachus waved off Silas's attempt to pay him and took his farewell, shoving the boat into the slip leading to the gulf. He shouted that he was headed for the docks at Thessalonica: "Back to business; good fortune to you!" they called out in their exchange of good-byes.

Silas looked at Archos. "I expected you to accompany Lysimachus, Archos. Are you delaying your return?"

"No, Deacon, I am not returning to Athens. But where is Adrianos?" Phoebe's nephew was the key to the trip through those upland thickets in the shadow of Olympos. All three of them were more than impatient to see him for the prospect that he might have brought food.

Rather quickly, almost suddenly, the shoreline fog began to lift, dissipating in the sun's waxing heat. In the clearing mist, they saw someone walking, carrying bundles and leading a donkey. Whoever it was, he saw them. Drawing closer to him, Silas and his companions noticed that the wiry, bald, red-bearded fellow seemed friendly. He hailed them: "Looking for Adrianos? Look no farther; good fortune is yours. I am he!"

Silas could not restrain his tongue. "Friend Adrianos, do you have any idea how much you resemble Paul?"

"No, and whose fault or worry might that be?" came the reply.

Silas joked that Paul had not fought for popularity in this district, adding the Paul had, from necessity, learned to create his own applause. "Oh, I do that, too," Adrianos remarked, bringing his hands together. "In fact, join me in applauding myself, in part for the excellent shore meal I have prepared for you. Come with me —back a few paces, and we will feed our bellies with freshly caught fish and a barley soup nicely garnished with herbs and hard breads." They laughed as they sat chatting on logs, sharing the meal Adrianos had prepared.

"We must start for Berea," he declared, "or else we will spend the night on the bear-ridden slopes of Mount Olympos." Then taking his new companions in tow, he directed them to start a small caravan up and westward.

During the late morning, they rescued an aged hunter who had drifted off the path, and they fed him from their supplies, joining him in a small repast of hard breads and cheese. Just before dusk, they all overcame their weariness again, cheering one another on, when Tobi heard two lost and injured boys, hurt and dirty from falling into a slough. Silas praised him for his part in the rescue, saying, "Tobi , you more or less single-handedly hoisted them out of the mud. Good man, Tobi!" Then the Deacon insisted that they push ahead: "Let's get out of reach of Olympos's shadow," he said Succeeding in that, they followed the passes, which sloped toward the destination the donkey and his four human companions sought. Next ahead lay the enormous range that made up Mount Vermion, lying off to the northwest as another of Greece's shadow builders but barely less exalted than noble Olympos.

FEASTING WITH THE DEACON

There, on Vermion's northeast slopes, the main road moved on to Edhessa, but it yielded a narrow side branch, a path. The path began in the low thicket at Berea's well; it escalated the pilgrim traveler's eyes through the scanty orchards in the village. Still further exploration of the scene brought into view the broken, low-lying clouds that that enclosed Mount Vermion. Vermion's rugged and menacing heights stood just west of the travelers' destination, Berea, which was finally at hand. At this point, Tobi took Silas's hand and smiled at the others as he reminded them, "I must catch a channel sailboat and get back to Corinth." It was not a goodbye, yet, as Silas said, "We do not know when we will see one another again. Thank you, Tobi. Go with God." The Cornicular gave each of them a hug, most lingeringly with the Deacon.

Then, as he turned from the view of the departing Tobi, Silas directed his eyes so his glance could commence that journey; it did not end; it went beyond. The journey would go far beyond Berea, to Heaven itself....

ARRIVAL AT BEREA

Silas fell to his knees. This moment deserved a prayer of thanksgiving, unvoiced praise and gratitude for the completion of one journey, the commencement of a new spiritual trek. He loved, too, the silence of such times. Adrianos interrupted the quiet invocation with a call of "Silas, Silas!" and the deacon upbraided himself, prodding his own ribs: 'One can pray and also continue climbing!'

Continuing the arduous climb, Silas called out, "Do we really know how to find Caleb's house? Ah-h, yes, we are breaking through these thickets. They grow along the river, just below Berea. We are close to the village." Late afternoon already; Adrianos and the others, although some were only half his age, had begun to complain of growing tired —all that lifting, pushing, carrying and continuing to carry.

Learning the location of their homes, they had accompanied the lads back to their families. That had meant a delay and diversion for their already difficult undertaking. But the men, especially those from Aquila's household, had agreed that the boys' distress required the attention Silas proposed.

Now it was necessary to get on with the search for their overnight lodging.

"Adrianos, did you hear me?"

"Oh, Caleb's house? I thought you knew we are not staying there tonight," Adrianos said. "Instead, Silas, we are to be guests of Gaius's overnight. Aunt Phoebe found out that he will be here for a few days longer. Since he will shortly take up his mission work in Thessalonica, several of his family members have already moved out of their lodgings here. Just Gaius himself and his wife, Eunice, have remained here in Berea. Didn't I tell you?"

"It doesn't matter, Adrianos; is he expecting us?"

"Certainly; both he and Caleb were told of our agreement to stay in Gaius' larger house, which is what Gaius wanted to offer you."

Some six furlongs ahead, just off the main road to Berea, a stone walkway led to the well-kept house where Gaius lived. At Silas's call, Gaius limped to the door, welcomed the travelers, and set them at a table with cakes and sweet pudding. Oh, what a treasured memory it would be: this soft, sweet and quiet entry into Berea! "Before I retire, please show me your little kitchen and food supplies, Gaius," Silas requested. "In the morning, I shall have to uphold my reputation, you know."

Healthy laughter and calls of 'Silas feeds!' forced Gaius to wait briefly before he could reply, observing the group romp through **Silas leads and Silas feeds; Among his many worthy deeds, The best is that our Silas feeds.** They repeated the gay chant in their wild dance until Gaius halted it and led his honored guest to the supply closet, agreeing to lie abed while Silas made breakfast the following morning.

Then, Silas went to the doorway, removed his petasos and pounded it on the post beside the entrance, raising a cloud of dust.... Thereupon, he turned and said a blessing to all before he sought out the room where he would spend the night. After he had pinched the candle and said his own thanksgiving and silent praises, the tired deacon fell asleep.

Even Silas slept late the following morning, but he had found the kindling, the pots and the ingredients he needed for a substantial feeding at Gaius' Berea house as the after-dawn mists broke. He presumed no one else was awake yet, but the host's voice from the doorway invalidated that presumption.

"This man cooked the best meal I ever ate when I stumbled through Corinth," Gaius proclaimed, announcing "Morning! Breakfast! Silas!," and his physical condition all at once.

"This man," Silas remarked pointing at his own face, "this man remembered Gaius as a fellow who prefers to sleep in companionship with the sun overhead; are you that Gaius? Or has your Eunice —"

FEASTING WITH THE DEACON

"His Eunice," interjected Eunice, who now sidled next to her Gaius, "his Eunice, Silas, has a bird's sense of daytime. Besides, we know the Corinthians who accompanied you want to start their return trip; add to that the fact that many of your future friends have begun to gather at our gate to see you."

"To see me? Who?"

"Well, Caleb, of course, who proposes to provide your lodgings —at least for a few days."

"As I recall, Phoebe said I was to use Caleb's home as long as I wished."

"Of course, you can speak to Caleb about those arrangements, but he runs a rather busy house —" Eunice started to explain, suffering an interruption from the doorway. Caleb had pushed his thin frame to the entrance; his eyes darting uneasily from face to face, he spoke on his own behalf. "Hello, Silas, yes I am the door-to-door cabinet maker. You remember me!"

"Caleb, of course; Caleb, do I make a problem for you by planning to lodge with you as I commence my preaching and start my mission here?"

"Not really, unless the presence of other guests bothers you," Caleb answered. With a nervous laugh, he continued, "I practice an open-house policy, Silas —especially when I leave on extended deliveries or when I go out for a supply of cabinet wood. You can expect to have a fairly noisy bedchamber, but friendly companions —some are very friendly," he added with a snort and a wink.

Silas, unsmiling, showed that he understood. Lifting the front brim of his petasos, he looked for Gaius, and across the room, Gaius looked at Silas, then beyond his face at the gathering crowd. Twelve to sixteen adults and children assembled behind Caleb's wiry shoulders. Gaius assessed their motivation and announced,"I assume you have made this welcome visit primarily to satisfy your curiosity. Yes, he is here; Silas is here. But, may I ask you, for the sake of this weary traveler, that you permit him to collect his thoughts in some privacy. You will all get to know him soon...."

"And probably find me tiring far too soon," Silas tossed in, blue eyes smiling. "But, Gaius, before you shoo away my future friends, let us share in a song, something I know well enough in Greek; how about the 'Gathering Song'?"

So, they all joined in, some knowing four or five verses, but all romping along with Silas in the refrain: **We open this ring, This circle, to sing, Circle and dance Sing, clap and dance —And all will be well, be well: *Ola kali.***

As they sang the Gathering Song a second time, Caleb interrupted Silas with a call to two women: "Come, you two lovelies, come and meet Silas, the new mission head. Silas, these two are very much my women, but you may as well get acquainted. This fireball is Zayda, my regular bedmate, who controls my life." Silas acknowledged Zayda with 'Zay-da', and a smile, then turned to the taller woman, touched her hand, and asked for an introduction by inquiring, "A—and may I have the pleasure?"

"Silas, welcome! I am Melana," she announced. "I administer some of the properties and oversee certain activities of the Proconsul here in Berea, but I do not dominate anyone's life, right, Zayda?"

Zayda shrugged, and Caleb responded by snorting his awkward-sounding snort.

They then looked away from Silas. As Silas held Melana's glance, he realized that he had always looked for Melana's face, he had always yearned to stroke her face, he had always sought to share in the strength God had given her body, And that he had always desired to sing the many songs Melana knew.

On that quiet morning in Berea, Silas was not bold enough to tell her about his claim on ALWAYS. It was Caleb who made insistent comments and pushed them into Silas's ear, displacing views Silas might have preferred to capture for his own eyes. Caleb was saying, "Whatever happened to that man, Paul, who was with you two or three years ago, when you came through Berea? The fellow who had such a thirst for wine that it seemed a problem? I want to talk to you about that, and I have some other questions."

"Caleb, I shall remember your question, but I have to deal with other matters, concerns that fit our mission plan. Enlarging our community: That matter is more urgent than Paul's whereabouts, I believe —certainly much more important than whether or not I lodge with you," Silas replied softly but firmly, observing Caleb's grudging look.

To capture the attention of the gathered group, Silas then raised his voice: "Good Morning, all! I am so glad to see this friendly outpouring of welcomes; they foretell sharing and mutual worship. We should all be grateful for that prospect. However, you should feel free to go along to

FEASTING WITH THE DEACON

your homes, or whatever else is expected of you at this hour. I shall be moving around, visiting villagers, in the next few days. As all of you Bereans should know, I loved you before I arrived back here. Now, say your prayers; counsel against evil; let love abound."

LAUDAMUS, SOPHIA!

The Lord of Lords keeps Wisdom inside a guarded well,
Gives us buckets and a map inscribed with Wisdom's spell;
Marks life's map with countless signs;
Hides a cue on every ledge; then Hands us strength to pull the lines in the well on Wisdom's edge.

*On the Sabbath or on other days that are set aside, take a place apart, with a few friends."—Epistle of Silas/

CHAPTER 3.

MARKETING IN THESSALONICA

Silas had hardly finished settling in at Berea when his new neighbors urged him to make the journey to Thessalonica. 'Go for supplies and a friendly visit with Gaius,' they suggested collectively. Silas took their suggestion, stopping to admire the great prominence of land and cascading waters at Edhessa, eating there at the home of Lysimachus, and arriving at Gaius' new home just after dusk on the second day.

Gaius had developed a more serious limp since Silas had seen him in Berea ('slipped on wet mud down by the sea,' he reported, waving it off) and joining Eunice, his wife, as those two old friends from Gaius' household embraced Silas warmly.

Eunice directed him to a quiet room set aside for prayer and guests. Silas slept well in Thessalonica —better than he had slept there three years ago when a partisan mob threatened him and Paul, chasing them away.

Awake the following morning, Silas concluded that he should make breakfast; in light of the quietness of the house, he muffled the clangs of the skillets and cooked rather silently. Later, ready with the breads and fruit conserves he had traded for in Edhessa, he left the cooking to find time for a silent hymn. He carried his prayers and contemplation to the north porch before the end of the first hour of the day after dawn.

It was then time to announce the meal, so he organized a one-man parade to call breakfast. He stomped, sang and knocked from door to door until the half dozen in Gaius' household began to gather in collective wonder.

"You must be Papa Gaius's friend Silas," called a lad of some eleven years.

Silas replied with 'Yes' in words, smiles and a brief dance, which he decorated with laughter. Soon, the entire sleepy-headed household had crowded around the fruit and baked items, and Silas had completed introductions.

When Gaius arrived on his crutch, several of his brood groaned, confessing they had eaten all of the tasty sweetbreads and teasing him, "Poor Deacon Gaius: You will spend a hungry day!"

Silas would have none of it. He opened another small basket and shared the most special breads of that Edhessan bakery and fruits with Gaius. "Deacon to deacon," he said. "Servant to servant." Gaius took his hand and held it firmly.

Before the third hour, Silas remarked, "I must go to the market, get these baskets filled with supplies, and head back to Berea before sunset — by tomorrow's dawn, latest, to arrive there for a special gathering I've planned for two days from now."

So, he took his directions and started toward the market. From the doorway, Gaius shouted, "Silas, you can get to Berea on time even if your marketing takes all day today. You are most welcome to spend the coming night in our home, if that also fits your plans".

"Thank you, my Brother, we shall see," Silas responded. On the way to the market, Silas found stalls of household goods, scarves, beads, and sandals, and bought two pairs of sandals. He told the shoemaker that he was newly arrived in the city and was surprised to learn that he had been mistaken for a local, hearing that "there are so many of you Jews here, running from Rome and from Jerusalem." He took that to signify the openness of the city to diversity ("Thank God!" he sang out) and had an internal vision of related problems and conflicts that might arise.

Meandering toward the food market, he found it vibrant with bargaining; blossoming with yellow melons, white squash, and purple plums. There was chattering in several tongues, some of them singing to lyres and flutes.

Surprises arose among the plums and peaches: In an uncharacteristic awkwardness, Silas stepped to his left while allowing one lingering look at the overripe plums on his right. His moves brought him close to a woman who stood locked between his shoulder and the intersection of two trays of fruit. Although he did not perceive the difficulty, she saw the imminent collision, and she stopped, leaning with her bosom serving as forward fencing. He did not sense this anatomical clash, but, to himself, muttered, "Those fruits would be very tasty now, but they would spoil before I arrive back in Berea."

Now it was the woman's turn to remark, "Oh yes, long before you would arrive in Berea," and she pulled him toward herself. "Why would you wish to go to that village when you can enjoy so many of life's riches here in the city?"

"Should you be offering so much to a stranger?" Silas asked. "Moreover, a stranger who is looking for others to join him chastely on the Way to spiritual bliss, eh?"

She made a dangerously seductive move and said, "You must be one of those who deny themselves playful ecstasies in order to claim some future fruit! Really, you are silly to take such a view, you know, when our touching bodies offer far more immediate joy than will ever come from the spaces behind our eyes. By the way, my name is Delilah, handsome one; are you my Samson?"

"Oh no, Delilah, but do not weaken," Silas urged. "Help strengthen me by moving back toward your home in —is it Sorek? —or your friend behind you, the other lovely woman. She stands now beside the melon rack."

The now-identified Delilah snarled in response and pushed him in the direction of the woman beside the melons: "You are so proud of your high mindedness that you will never take time to enjoy life's hot little cushions, such as I offered to you —and I am **not** the Sorekkan Delilah, no. But go ahead; go to this woman. I know her. She is not my friend; she is nothing but a gardener!"

Now, Silas, embarrassed, hopped to the right, realizing that he was not being sufficiently watchful for the woman shopping at the melon stand. He stepped back to give both of them distance. His glance met hers slowly and then, diverting, he felt her glance speed along his bearded face. Gentle glances at first, faces still sober. Then two smiles started; two smiles formed and a new brightness glowed in their eyes, hers black and embedding an indelible reflection of his eyes of blue. Delight came in delayed recognition, joined by a sudden warmth —a warmth rushing as the path of brightness rushes ahead of a clearing cloud and shoves aside the shadows.

To herself, Melana observed that he was almost as tall as she. Silas absorbed the full set of darker colors that painted her: black hair, eyes too dark to name, and skin the shade of well-baked bread. From these, a radiance charged at him, and she said, "Remember me? I am Melana." She smiled and an energizing richness flowed from her smile and her eyes. To himself, he spoke: 'Not since Pentecost have I suffered such a blow.' He braced himself to withstand it.

"Melana! How could I fail to recognize you? Melana!" He nodded. The sound of her name in the air pressed against his breathing. "Melana," he inquired, "can you help me select the best?" He held firmly to the frame of the fruit stall. She moved closer, her hand extended into the air, bracing him by an implied offer of support. As he recovered, they both pretended to laugh, dismissing the storm.

She spoke again, confirming his identification: "You are the blue-eyed Berean who always hunts for the best, finds the best, and gives it away, they say." She interrupted her narrative to laugh lightly, then caught herself and made a silencing motion toward her lips. Soberly, she resumed, "The word is getting around the village —including everyone in Berea. You should be pleased, Silas, as I am ."

"You are?" He accepted the entire report as if she had intended a perfect compliment. She could not have done better if she had laid out a map to his heart!

"Yes, I have a stake in Berea and actually expect to stay there, although I am today only the gardener for the proconsul —wherever he is stationed.... If you, the new deacon, wonder what brings a Berean gardener to Thessalonica —-"

"Yes, I wonder, and you have started to counter the question my wonderment asks, I assume," Silas interrupted, further capturing the opportunity by inserting, "To be sure, I am the servant deacon, the missioner: Silas... Melana!"

"I am pleased to meet you again, Deacon Silas! Now, if I may, let me admit the proconsul's desire to make extra monies selling the excess abundance of vegetables from his garden. I load a donkey and cart and market many of our surpluses here in Thessalonica, since the Berean demand is not great enough to fill a small bag of coins. We can make a tidy profit here. Moreover, the proconsul is sympathetic to your work, as his wife and I are among the faithful believers in Berea. He encourages me to take a portion of the proceeds for your mission work."

"Great glory! The Romans do know how to make an institution operate, don't they?" Silas said. "Perhaps," he suggested, "you would also have some room in your cart on the return trip; would you consider a passenger?"

FEASTING WITH THE DEACON

"Oh, how bold you are, Silas! Did you not expect that I had set space aside in the cart for purchases I should make here?" Melana laughed lightly, then soothed the small mocking with, "I tease too much; it was a common practice in the household where I grew up. Of course, Deacon, there will be room for you; I will change my plans a bit and rearrange the cart and the goods. Also let me make a second suggestion," Melana hurried on with her wind of words.

"I can foresee it already, I believe —you know where to find plums that will ripen for enjoyment in Berea."

"You are too wise," Melana teased. "I can understand that you may be a prophet, Silas, but I was not prepared for a mind reader!"

"If I qualify for that role, young woman, it appears we have forged harmonious thoughts today."

"Yes, Silas, and I hope you will agree to join me and my donkey and a basket of ripening plums tomorrow at about the second hour after dawn. My cart will be at the corner where Alexandros Street meets the Via Egnatia."

"Melana, I will surely be prompt and ready to leave. Shall I tell my friends here that we will go by way of Edhessa? I have friends there, a household of believers. You understand?"

Melana nodded. "I am ready to inquire into some of the matters you have brought to Berea. Going by way of Edhessa would permit us to look into them, thank you."

Melana: the name rang nicely as he sang it, walking back to Gaius' house. Melana… calling it shaped a view of her face, and it was a most friendly portrait he held among his thoughts as he composed his evening prayer and drifted to sleep.

'Melana', he said to himself as he awoke the following morning; yes, his life could accommodate the sound and significance of those three syllables. 'I can accept that she may have received the name because of her darker complexion, but I will name her by her own name because of Mele, like honey, hoping honey will be a part of our partnership, however it progresses.'

It was a night for postponing sleep in Thessalonica. Not to forego it. Silas simply postponed it.

"Silas." Melana spoke the name as if to test the air, and the word brought a view of his smile, as it had brightened the fruit stall in Thessalonica, across the ripening plums. Silas: 'What-was-wished,' if she remembered correctly that dialect's vocabulary. Well, she would see; she made no assumptions about this, but 'I do like what I saw behind those eyes…perhaps, it was the way they were shaded by the brim of his peasant hat. Sometime, I must consider making a petasos for myself', she suggested, as she snuffed the oil lamp's flame, letting sleep displace images of the encounter at the marketplace.

Morning brought back a thought of making a hat, and she jumped from bed to try to expel foolish thoughts. But they stuck and would not unstick. She then said, "But perhaps it is not a foolish thought, Melana."

And each of them found the corner at the entrance to the Via Egnatia at about the designated time. She told him that she had no name for her donkey, urging it on with a call of 'Go, friend!' and they were off to stop at Edhessa on the way to Berea. Silas observed that it is a blessing to have a sturdy donkey as a friend, and they chatted about the good weather, as all travelers do.

At Thessalonica's western gate, Roman sentries stopped the travelers. Ignoring Melana, who was regarded as 'only a woman driver,' an officer moved toward Silas, saluting. "Hail, I see the Imperial eagle on the vehicle. My respects, and my request to see your safe passage paper." Jumping from the open rear of the cart, Silas admitted that his Latin was too poor to carry on, also that the vehicle and donkey were the Berean proconsul's.

As he started to point to her, Melana showed the officer her passage paper and began an easy conversation with the sentries, chiding them a bit. "You assumed that I was only the driver, perhaps less! Perhaps only a driver's helper, because I am a woman, dark-skinned at that! If you will examine your records, you will find I have managed the Berean proconsul's affairs for two years —since he relocated from Alexandria. I am now his gardener, my choice."

"Your forgiveness, please," pleaded the sentry, waving them on.

Silas could not restrain his awe: "I admire your effectiveness, Melana. Thank you for rescuing me from an awkward attempt in Latin. I am only recently able to relax in the Greek Koine, as now, and to exercise classic Greek. Latin —well, I stagger through Latin as a schoolboy from Jerusalem once did. My father, who knew Latin well, emphasized Hebrew dialects, and did not teach me or my late brother the command of conversational Latin, just a few slang phrases and curses —ugly little devices that often cause trouble," Silas commented.

"But with the advantage of adding some color!" Melana reminded him. "And I hope you would have allowed me to assert my place and position, even if you spoke perfect Latin."

"I learned long ago to try to open every opportunity for people to shine, to blossom and to grow, Melana. My mother, Miriam, was a woman, I like to remind friends! And most of my happiness in life has come from friendships with bright and beautiful women." "Well, I am impressed by the upbringing and the results. It surprises me that you did not marry; that's true, is it not?"

"Melana, I have given much thought to marriage and supporting a household, and yet the whole set of necessary and sufficient causes never quite assembled to collaborate at a given time. For one thing, the reliability of fortune is not high for a person whose trade is that of a scribe. Yet I have continued to consider the married state, a station that Paul argues against as if it were unnatural. So, let me say that I am not shopping, but I am certainly willing. In fact, one of the reasons for going back by way of Edhessa is that my friend, Mauros, who lives there, has a sister whom he wants me to meet. So?"

Melana smiled; "You are so frank and open, Silas. I have not known a man like you on those points."

The trip to Edhessa permitted them to get acquainted on many points: one being that Silas 'grew up in the Jordan Valley, son of a Roman officer and scribe, Titus Gaddiel Lucanius, and my mother, Miriam, daughter of a landed Valley family.' "Together," he went on, "my parents had elected to arrange for my father to detach himself from the army and to join my mother in establishing a market garden farm on her family land. There, they cultivated, harvested and prepared for sale a variety of green vegetables for the officers' commissary. Hence, my interest in food supplies and cooking,' he admitted.

"Oh yes, we Bereans have quickly grown aware of your skill with pots and pans and herbs and spices," she confided. "From the aromas that arise, we know more about your success in the kitchen than we know about your mission. But I am eager to learn more!"

"Excuse me, but I am not certain of the meaning of your comment, Melana. Do you mean that you wish to know more about the mission or the kitchen?" They enjoyed a laugh, and he continued, "I suspect you know more than I about kitchens, so may I tell you about the noblest mystery that mankind has ever shared with the Infinite God?"

"Silas, I am deeply interested in learning about it, since we had so little discussion of the nature of God and less about the rewards of a good life. I may say that I have seen very few examples of the virtuous life and even fewer examples of how good people react to evil."

Silas did not lean eagerly into the continuation of the little sermonette, saying, "Your sincere curiosity should take longer than a lecture, so I will only begin today. I am going to start telling you about the forever news and the loving forgiveness the Master taught. More, as we go along and as you request it. Is that satisfactory?"

"Certainly, Silas," Melana replied, "I have begun —along with other Bereans —to become mindful of the richness of spirit and the songs and laughter at the gatherings around the little hut you have borrowed for community meetings. Now, traveling with you on this smooth Macedonian highway, I can listen to your description of your work and what you call the Word. Yes, I listen to you, unbelieving and yet almost believing, almost aflame with acceptance and yet doubtful," she ended.

Briefly, they meditated, praising and (in silent prayer) asking for illuminations —that those illuminations might reveal the face of Wisdom to them, Wisdom that would bring elements of the Highest Love.

As they reached the outskirts of Edhessa, Silas told her how they would find the two houses where they would spend the night and the easiest route to the barn where the donkey could be fed and appropriately rested. He took care of those chores while she arranged their lodgings.

Having taken care of accommodations, Silas suggested that they stop for a repast at a taverna. She did not resist.

They discovered that the household of Mauros no longer held an unmarried sister. In fact, that very evening, Mauros's wife was serving as a midwife for her sister's labor during her first childbirth. Thus, although they had adequate lodgings, they would have to take care of their own needs for companionship over dinner and the rest. They thanked Mauros and found an inn, with a taverna serving those who were not lodging at the inn. That fit their needs quite well.

FEASTING WITH THE DEACON

Together, they ate a small supper followed by spice cakes and a glass of local red wine. "Now, tell me the story of Melana," Silas insisted, even as they sipped the wine.

"Silas," she began, "first, look at the shade of my skin —an inheritance from my beautiful and very dark mother. According to the best account I can find, she was brought to Alexandria from the border country, near Ethiopia, to slave for Roman officials. However, she became the concubine of my father, who served as a senior officer in the Alexandrine guard until some 15 years ago, when he was killed by Nile river pirates in an attack on his barracks."

"So sorry that you suffered that loss.... How did you come to continue to work as a household servant, since you are also a Roman citizen?"

"Silas, let me proceed. Mother died when I was born; I was fed by another woman —a wet-nurse in the community. Father also died when I was very young, and I was probably expected to wander back into the empty pathways that my dark sisters have been walking for many years."

The tavern keeper brought small bowls of raisins and nuts; then she asked them if they would like another glass of wine. The Deacon and his new friend smiled, agreeing to the second glass.

By the end of their third glass of wine, the hour had grown late, and they concluded that they could halt their review of origins, although Silas challenged her with hopes that they might soon draw the curtains even wider. Melana agreed, adding that "an examination of destinies could prove even more interesting than that of our ill-documented origins."

Silas now knew that Melana had been adopted by the household of the proconsul who had been transferred to Berea two years ago. As they spoke further, he learned that she had been tutored in languages, serving as translator to and from Greek, Hebrew, Coptic and Latin; she had been given charge of kitchen and garden in Alexandria, a post that the proconsul had reserved for her in Berea as well.

"But," she confided, "I have begun to consider a married life, if the right person comes along. I knew Caleb, when we were both children in Alexandria, but we have merely followed our natural curiosity derived from our childhood friendship —certainly nothing more. I was somewhat surprised to find him in Berea; he had left Alexandria in some haste, about eight years ago."

"Well, we all have to move along in haste, just to do our duties," Silas observed, without helpful reference. "Now, our duty is to tie up for the night, get rest, and go on to Berea tomorrow, true?"

Melana agreed. In their separate quarters, they slept in small clouds atop newly minted prayers. At dawn they met to move along to Berea, where they arrived before dusk. They had spent the entire day going through one another's library of life, and both books —hers and his —gave instruction, entertainment and inspiration. She looked for the next chapter; he, for the next paragraph.

As they separated to go to their own homes, Silas declared, "An important friendship has begun here. I will work to meet its obligations, Melana."

"I shall count on that and hold you to it in the time ahead, Silas. My debt has started to grow, too, and I have not left a creditor unpaid, not ever. Now, good night. Include me in your prayers, as you are in my best thoughts."

A mosaic of new impressions and delightful images decorated Silas' meditations and hallelujahs. He pondered the images that interrupted his prayers, bringing views of Melana's face and shadow-sounds of her voice. Mindful again of Melana's roots at Alexandria, he recited in silence:

'Ah, Egypt! Out of Egypt a vigorous grapevine, whose each new branch brings nourishment and a bright spirit.'

He fell asleep in Berea; his voyage to sleep journeyed across musings over the Berean vineyard. Similar dreams visited both of them after sleep blessed them. Dreams came to him with haunting intrusions by the face of Caleb. Neither of them spoke of that when they next met....

RETROSPECTIONS ON MEETING MELANA

I.

At Two Years

Now, you are 'two': a pair of cheering candles stands Atop your decorated cake, And your dark eyes hide milk-fed kitten memories, Memories that in some distant future time May count both ecstasy and ache. Merry, merry child of joy —Melana, merry Miss! How sweet your nape of neck, Where Rufulus ———but three —So shyly leaves a kiss.

FEASTING WITH THE DEACON

II.
At Six Years

You are an eaglet; Your voice rings bells in heaven and enchants my ear; As you speak, your wisdom Runs ahead of this, your seventh year; But when you shift from girlish humming To intone sweet songs of joyous praise, Greying Alexandria laughs and counts the gifts That shall emerge in future days.

III
At Seventeen

Some see sunshine in your lovely hair, Others prize your sculpted ear that nobly rounds its space, But I find gardens in your lively eyes And long to touch the flowers in your face.

IV.

Melana to Her Love: `I am dark'My face I see behind your piercing eyes.That sudden printing of my brow On scrolls within your mind Reflects my own; we both rejoice in this surprise; And yet, I sense our fear, more than either can allow —Is it because my skin is dark? Come now! Do I dare hope you see the overlay of soul With vision some term `color-blind'? `Yes,' you reply; "Yes," you assert, in all the songs you sing.

And quietly, My sounds of "yes" come echo-echo-echoing.

CHAPTER 4.

LOCAL WOMAN MARRIES CHIEF OF MISSION

(Melana is 31, born on July 13 of her birth year; Silas is 47.)

"Observe, dear cousins and loved friends: Prayers that join many minds multiply their blessings."

Epistle of Silas/

On her wedding day, Melana wakened to the smell of food and the nearby noise of hammering. Hammering came from Silas's house nearby. The smell of food arose from her own little kitchen, where Gaius' wife was warming a sweet honey cake and waiting for a collation of herbal leaves to become a steeped tea. "I am so fortunate!" Melana exclaimed to her household, "Such rich fortune to have loving friends who will brew teas and make sweet breads to decorate my table and favor my tongue."

Gaius heard Melana as she completed her preparations for the day, and he added, "Later, when you and Silas complete your promises, there will be a tasty serving table for all to praise: cooled red wine, raisins, nuts, figs from Antioch, and much love."

Silas's house. There her husband-to-be sat admiring the *huppa* and the small table that would stand beside them in the ceremony Silas had prepared from recollections out of his youth in Jerusalem.

She arose, as she observed the rest of the village had already done; those who did not know certain answers had already posed certain matching questions:

Where could Berea find enough tables to hold all the cakes?
Where could the fruits and the flowers find room?
How could such wealth of happiness loom?
Bereans will celebrate a wedding.

Who is marrying? Melana is —Melana, who had lived in the gatehouse of the proconsul's garden, on the crest of the hill.

She will be the bride. Silas, who heads the new mission, will marry her and will bring her back married to the little house allotted him, the house that almost sits inside the mountain spring. They will marry in the presence of their friends, to their own increased blessing and to the glory of God.

Look at the crowd! In addition to Gaius, who brought his family from Thessalonica, Phoebe and Prisca arrived from Corinth; Prisca's Aquila, she reported, has suffered an attack of illness but sent his love.

Timothy came by way of everywhere. "Yes, I hope you do not have to answer to the prefects in Thessalonica for the fixed addresses of your guests, at least not this one," Timothy challenged. "I guess I have to tell you about being stopped at the edge of Berea by an old fellow who wanted to know where I was headed; I told him 'to Heaven.' He warned me dryly, 'Not on that donkey, you won't.' I laughed so hard, I nearly fell off the jackass I was riding, but —as you see, I did get here, still on the road to Heaven."

Picking up on the humor, Melana observed, "Timothy, your serious countenance, which seems overdone to many of us, gives us opportunities to joke at your expense. I wonder how many of the old fellow's friends are laughing at his version of that story over at the Hideaway Tavern." Again, a roar of laughter, such that someone bumped Prisca, who spilled some wine on Caleb's new tunic. Caleb backed away as if to protect his bright-colored garments, and growled —just as Prisca noticed her misstep and apologized for the accident. Again, Caleb growled.

"Oh-ooh!" Silas interjected, stepping in front of Caleb, in an obvious move to cut him off and to perpetuate the merrier mood that instilled the gathering crowd of friends.

"It seems to me," Silas said, "we might as well begin with the serious business, allowing that your light-hearted tales have already caused some sloshing." Melana smiled in happy assent.

"Friends," Silas announced in his 'crier's voice' —"Friends, Melana and I welcome you to our wedding. We have constructed it from our own phrasing, woven in some of our own songs, borrowed some Macedonian dances to blend with the Judean and Alexandrine games of our childhood days. For our benefit and joy, as well as yours, we have preserved those markings that remind us of who we are."

FEASTING WITH THE DEACON

Melana took advantage of the brief pause to add, "My lovely Silas has built the *huppa* that will cover us as we pledge our love to one another and our thanksgiving to God. We pray for children, and we have already recited the *berakhot* prayer that asks blessings on this gathering. I have to add that this mixture reminds me of the ways Silas develops his recipes, borrowing and blending all that stands within reach, promising to make the texture or the taste of the dish more interesting!"

Caleb shouted, "What did you prepare for the wedding supper, Silas?"

"Oh, you shall see," the Deacon replied. "I suspect I spent as much time over my victuals as you did, Caleb! Now, I would suggest Melana and I should proceed with our vows."

With Gaius, Phoebe and Timothy serving as formal attendants, Silas and Melana began their pledges somewhat informally; between the figs and the cakes, Silas told her: "You are my Light, the daughter of Wisdom. Wherever you are, my life has no shadows."

"Silas, You are my decorator, the son of Wisdom. You beautify me; you build a temple for our love; flowers line the walls of the temple; the flowers will never wilt."

"Because You are the vessel of love, I am also the vessel of love. I am the generator of love, and you are the leaven and spice of love," Silas reminded her.

"Go on!" someone from the gathering called. "Melana," Silas said, speaking in a confiding whisper, "you are truly beautiful. I must say, *Nigra estis, sed pulchra*! May I tell you that?"

"Ha-haa!" Melana softly laughed. "Of course, You may —you with the magic words; Solomon's words, really, if I correctly recall. Black-am-I and beautiful; yes, so I am.... So I feel, and more so today —thinking on the words of *Shir-ha-Shirim*, the great Song of Songs. Oh, Silas! Could we celebrate my dark skin in the meal today: dark fruits, richly dark and joined with blood-red wine? Should I blush shy in making this thought so public?"

"Thanks to your skin coloring," he murmured, "your blushes are less noticeable than those of certain fair-skinned persons within our hearing." Aloud, Silas announced that they were marrying among their friends, telling them, "We shall share many things with you; today I foresee an eggplant stew, with peppered herbs. We will `end the meal with dark grapes and plump cherries, opaque with their substance, deeply purpled in hue."

"Get on with it! Be married!" another call came.

Thus they went about reminding one another of the solemn promises they would make, to care and share wealth and worries until he or she might die. Then, they simply made those promises, voicing Mother Esther's words for the *dat wa din* —the Jewish custom and manner. When they had both spoken the pledge in Hebrew, they also proceeded through the words that adhered to the Greek *nomo kai tropo* —after all, they were in Greece! Following these sober pledges, they stood quietly for a time in prayer under the yellow huppa. In the gathered silence, Silas said in Hebrew, "Wherever you go, I go too." Then Melana recited the same words in Coptic, and Silas took those words from the legend of Ruth into the Greek of his neighbors, the Koine; finally Melana sang at him: *Ubi tu, ego. Ubicumque: wherever!*

'That will surely satisfy the Romans!' someone shouted. Thus, it seemed they had satisfied themselves, their observers and guests, and especially Timothy. They thereby satisfied themselves that they had surely satisfied God. Silas began to drum a rhythm and moved his feet in a country dance, extending his arms invitingly as their guests began to chant a song. Silas saw Melana rise from her stool and begin a solitary dance, which he had already modeled. He shouted to her, "My Love, we must never dance or eat alone. Come let us dance to our own music. Keep it moving!" She smiled and embraced the air as she ran toward him. Then, taking the hands of friends who shortly encircled them, they entered that ring and pulled one another along laughing.

The chain of merrymakers wound through Berea's sloping hillside streets for the better part of the afternoon. Melana shone like a star; Silas beamed as he had not since he was a boy in Judea.

From time to time, a dish appeared on a community table along the way, and rather rapidly its contents vanished, but shortly afterward another Berean stew or dessert would appear on another table down along the dancers' path. The dancers progressed in happiness through the small village along the Triple River, the *Tripotamos* branch of the Aliakmon, there in Berea.

One hundred years earlier, Rome's Pompey, the conquering General, had spent the winter in that very village with a Macedonian dancer and entertainer. **This** celebration was significantly different, and moving in every meaning of the word. Silas and Melana shouted, "So moving!" and kept the momentum for hours.

FEASTING WITH THE DEACON

"Leave them to themselves," called Gaius as the partying moved toward the house where Caleb and Zayda lived. Although Silas followed Melana toward their own new home, the other party-goers grew quickly aware of the quarreling from Caleb's hut that polluted the village air. Other Bereans knew that his comparisons, contrasting Zayda and Melana, had led to vicious cuts from Zayda's sharp tongue and a string of oaths and curses from Caleb.

Most of the partying turned away and became admiration for the happy skip-dancing of Silas and Melana, as the newly married couple encircled one another along the sunlit Berean hillside.

Nearing their home, Silas turned to Melana, and their eyes said it all. Love, love, love.... How blessed to be so loved; how lovely to be so blessed! Tonight would set the example; there was no need to say the little speech he had composed and half rehearsed for this moment; the moment framed the future for a multitude of joys, a concentricity of feasts. Thank God for all of this, he thought. "Thank God for all of this," said Melana.

He opened the door to the house and turned toward her in the doorway. He reached for her hand. Suddenly, Melana's arms surrounded him, as she picked him up and headed for their bedchamber. His hat —the new petasos he had bought in Thessalonica——fell off, as did one sandal, but Melana kept going, her considerable strength providing the means for translating her bridegroom from a standing position to prone.

He was quickly bed-borne, thanks to his well-built bride. "Oh what a journey!" Silas shouted, with a great laugh.

"More traveling yet tonight," replied Melana, realizing that both of them had a less than perfect understanding of the events to come. "Is it not appropriate to pray at a time like this?" she inquired.

"If we offer thanks and say a quick Amen, it would seem quite appropriate. Do you know a very short prayer?" Silas asked, sporting a grin —somewhat impish for a deacon.

"Oh, you! You have such a twinkle, my darling. Thank God I can see it!" she admitted.

"That will do, Melana. Thank God for the landscape and lights I can now admire. Praise God," Silas added in some haste, as the temperature increased in their lodging on the hillside in Berea.

Silas was first crackling fire;Melana was first a warm hearth.Swept up by an exchange of kisses, They start a miraculous ride, Astride the body's miracles, flying on tongues of flame; Soaring toward the tops of Mount Vermion, They do not suffer cooling on its upper slopes tonight. Tonight's flight assumes the warmth of a thermal wind, Soaring into the furnace gate. Do not step back from the furnace. Stay close Within the scorching furnace fires. Enjoy the deep burning. Pop and jump, romp and tear the bedding, Ignite the gowns, kiss the hot roundnesses. Enclose the flaming lance;Let it fill and gorge the oven with its wholesome heat. Let the warmth linger. Let it scamper through her softness.Hold to the heat of this first loving; Keep his body-maps well in mind. Do not forget the paths Around her breasts and down her brown belly; You shall move along those avenues again. Now, sleep in the snug-warm blankets of your delight; You will waken in the afterglow of those singular fires you feed.

`Good night, Melana! Good night, Silas!'

/Our patterns urge our outward reach by touch, by glance, in friendly speech.../Sign on Silas and Melana's doorway.

"Oh, what a morning! Silas-Shiza ——most loving, you are. And look! Sweet cakes and fruits for breakfast. Someone has left them for us at the door, and it is late —already the third hour, I believe, looking at that sun arriving from Thessalonica."

"Melana, get your body back here where it belongs! I shall prepare to feast off those dark mountains when you lie on your back. Having such a feast to enjoy, how might I then keep my appetites sorted?"

"My handsome Silas, do not fret. We Alexandrian women know a way to feed all appetites," Melana told him, and she whispered some great Egyptian secret into his ear, causing laughter and much more loving. And that was the first morning of the marriage of Melana and Berea's deacon. It marked another of the deacon's feasts, and his first understanding of Coptic ribaldry.

Four months later, Melana's dark-skinned belly began to show an enlarged roundness and a heaviness that she chose not to hide. In that lovely aspect, she paraded her first baby around Berea's paths and side streets long before it wore swaddles. However, one day, in her fifth month, she was ac-

FEASTING WITH THE DEACON

costed by a familiar voice: "Hey, lady, you could have been so blessed long ago!"

"Caleb! Caleb, You ruffian!" Melana rebuked, shaming her old friend from Alexandria. "Cease and show your proper upbringing."

"I am quite well brought up, Melana, and would have fathered your child while still in Alexandria, certainly by the time I found you again here in Berea, years before your holy Silas arrived."

"I shall ignore that remark, Caleb," Melana said, "and I do not welcome your intrusion into my life in such a manner."

"You wound me, dear old friend and more, you have always ignored or stabbed me," Caleb sniveled. "I am disappointed in the narrow view our so-called Christian soldier-lady has adopted from her newly adopted creed and newly bedded husband."

"That will be enough, and I shall pray for some repair and rearrangement in both your speech and your ways," Melana said, going on toward her home.

CHAPTER 5.

OLD BONES IN THE CLOSET

\"Hunger for new ways to give praise; find them; follow them."- Epistle of Silas/

I have a reputation for rearranging parts of both Berea and Alexandria," Melana claimed. After but a few months of married life, she had proved she could assure variety in the little stone house that stood above the creek. "Also," she continued, "I have convinced Silas to enjoy the spice of change."

'Convinced?' More accurately, Melana had induced a habit, an added belief, in her new groom's outlook. Following a series of pleasurable and astonishing acts by Melana, Silas considered pleading for someone to arrange a surprise for her. If a magician could reverse the flow of the Aliakmon River, or if a sorcerer might make rocks float in it, such demonstrations might astonish her. Melana appeared to find enough pleasure in amazing and bewildering him. Easy for her!

For example, one morning in the first week of their marriage, he mistook the rattling of utensils as her preparation of an elaborate meal. Investigating on behalf of his appetite, he found she had simply arranged pans to form a letter or letters of the alphabet.

Depending on the aspect that faced him as he looked at it from across the room, it was the **sigma/samekh/Σ** for Silas or the **mu/mem/M** for Melana!

ΜΣΜΣΜΣΜΣ   "Fortunately, we own only a limited number of pans," cracked Silas.

Other days, he would come into the cooking area following a long period of total quiet only to discover she had sliced, stewed and served a feast for them. In that way she worked songs of life into noise and silence, but he simply laughed without revealing the special hold she had placed on his imagination.

After eight days of marriage, the newly wed pair had quarreled once and made peace six times. "It appears peace will win here," Silas said over grapes and honeyed bread that morning, just as a caller arrived at the door, grunting for attention. In recognition, Silas responded, his voice strong, "Caleb! You have come alone?"

"Yes, Abba Silas, did you expect a legion?" Attempting humor, Caleb continued, "You must realize that Bereans do not prolong the celebration of wedding feasts. We have work to do." Then he muttered, "But it is your marriage to Melana that has brought me here." He paused, and Silas stepped back from him to inspect his countenance as he continued, urging, "Silas, can we go somewhere, for a very private talk?"

"Why, yes —you are not going to threaten me, are you?" Silas inquired, standing in a pose that left no doubt about Caleb's comparatively weaker physique. They both laughed, each in his own perspective on the matter.

Silas peeked back through the doorway, turning as he called, "Melanasha, Caleb and I have gone on a short walk to examine some rocks."

She acknowledged the message, sweeping her arms forward in an embrace of loving benediction: "Back before dusk?"

"Before dusk, I'm certain," Silas nodded, not realizing how much an examination of rocks can challenge the understanding. Caleb reached into a fold of his tunic and took out a handful of raisins and nuts. "Here, have a snack," he offered Silas. "We have a climb ahead of us."

"Yes, I see, Caleb, but climbing has been my lot and choice for many past years, many past miles."

"Speaking of the past," Caleb ventured, "I have been wondering about your origins.... What upbringing produced a religious rebel with such gentle ways? Tell me more about yourself, Abba, and how you got into your trade; whence your ambition?"

Silas smiled and plunged into his reply: "I will not resist answering you, Caleb, but ask you to hold off calling me 'Abba'; I aim to be the deacon, the servant of this community —not its father, and I doubt that you regard me as a parent. Your questions pluck at me; where are they heading? Are they grounded in caring and charity? More important to this climb, will their answers fit your need —your own search?"

Caleb shrank back, as if to say, 'Forget it, Silas.' Noticing the reaction, Silas said, "Let me accept that you have some outcome in mind when you

FEASTING WITH THE DEACON

ask my origins, and I assume that you intend to be helped by my answer. Accordingly, I want to tell you I was trained to be a scribe but also to cultivate the land and tend crops. My ambitions were to serve others, but above all else, to be able to prepare a meal for the hungry from the fruits of my garden."

"But of course," replied Caleb, "you are always feeding and serving foods. I suspect you believe you are someone special or at least specially marked for the work you carry out."

"I sensed a call to the Way, to this service, at about the time of the Master's final ministry around Jerusalem…. Caleb, I heard him; I heard him sing. Oh, how Jesus could sing!" A long pause followed, awkward to Caleb. Silas added, "There, I have said it; it helps to define me. Does it help you define our relationship, our friendship?"

"You dare me to say 'yes,' and I must tell you that it helps, Silas."

"Well, then, Caleb, let me offer you some honey breads that I made and brought along this morning; they may also help, and they remind me of the sweets and cakes at last week's wedding party. Remember that?"

"Indeed. Thanks for the breads… Silas, since you have mentioned the wedding, permit me to say that what I want to discuss with you greatly concerns Melana. There! Did I get your attention, Deacon?"

"Proceed; but be direct and do not tell me some old rumor baked in the Berean edile's kitchen."

"No, it is not a rumor, and the kitchen was in Alexandria. You know that Melana —"

"Of course, Caleb," Silas interrupted, saying, "I know my wife was a child in Alexandria; she told me that on the day we met. But, what further —?

"One further thing is that I meant to tell you earlier that your old partner, Mark, came to Alexandria at about the time I left. He was stirring up the city's synagogues with his preaching but not very successful in his attempts to convert the crowds that came around."

"Oh? Caleb, what do you —?"

"Silas, Mark was not too successful in his work; made very slow progress; his command of Greek —not nearly as good as yours —his fell short, and Mark did not speak Coptic at all. I think his Coptic was 'Pretend Coptic'. He seemed to have depended on his command of Latin to carry him, but Alexandrians are a Greek community and so he was not able to keep the audience he drew, except for the few who also spoke Hebrew. And —"

"Caleb, Mark will fulfill his mission! It takes some time; I think he will be regarded a heroic missionary; he has many gifts, many talents. But you have let your story drift, and you, too, are close to losing your audience. Does Alexandria matter so much, that you take me away to this quiet thicket?"

Caleb motioned him to stop, and they turned to sit on a large rock that dominated the slope of Mount Vermion above Berea. Silas sat on the rock. In the silence, he looked down on Berea as if in a reverie. He motioned Caleb to move beside him, to sit with him on the rock. Caleb joined the deacon but seemed in low spirits as he did so. He arranged his cloak to cushion himself and positioned himself to assure that he would not have to face the sun or Silas, as they continued.

Resuming the conversation, Caleb muttered, "Silas, I conclude that you resent the time subtracted from your morning with Melana."

"Well, Caleb, what will you say that can equal the treasure I am missing?"

"Listen, Silas. Do not interrupt, and I will try to finish this task I have given myself. I was also born in Alexandria, born a Jew; I am the son of an accountant who served one of the resident prefects. To increase our income, he arranged for Mother to nurse other infants at her breast, for a fee —what the Greeks call a wet nurse."

"When I was about two years old, Mother nursed a dark-skinned daughter of a widowed proconsul, a baby who is today your wife. Her father arranged for her to receive the care reserved for the aristocracy, and we seldom saw one another because we grew up in different parts of Alexandria. Because my mother served as a hired wet-nurse for several baby girls —as well as baby boys —I was carefully instructed in the prohibition called *radah*."

"Radah?" Silas inquired. "I am not acquainted with it."

As Caleb proceeded, he spoke slowly, as if chewing his words, laboriously transferring the lore of the Southern desert, the nomad culture, into Silas' understanding and his familiarities. "*Radah* in that world names a taboo," Caleb declared. "It describes a relationship and a forbidden closeness between a man and a woman who nursed from the same breast. It does not allow such breast-brother relationships to lead to intimacy of marriage; *radah* would deny marriage to the pair".

FEASTING WITH THE DEACON

Silas remarked that "*Radah* obviously might, by prohibiting it, might actually encourage a desire for the forbidden fruit."

"Oh yes, Silas," Caleb agreed "and when I realized that it would yield just that result in my case, I left Alexandria and came here some four years ago."

"So-o-o-o!" Silas inserted. "When Melana came as a result of the proconsul's relocation somewhat later, the prospect threatened —should I say 'fascinated' you again, true? I recall your eagerness to tell me all about yourself when Paul and Timothy were here with me the first time," Silas recalled, adding, "I did not imagine that something like this was agitating you. I suppose you want me to tell Melana that I know.... Caleb, does Melana know all these details?"

"I am not certain that she knows her wet nurse was my dear mother. Yes, she would likely be aware of *radah*, but Melana would not know that I have ached for her through the years," came Caleb's weak reply.

"Ached? You have ached? Surely not in loneliness! The village lore points to the intensive activity you have promoted in your bedroom. Living with Zayda (do you plan to marry Zayda someday?) —living with Zayda, but running through the alphabet quite irresponsibly, they say: Azubah, Berneice, Gorgo, Doris,...Rezia —Yes, likely each, a true *rezia*; a true delight, delights, one-at-a-time.... Should I go on?"

"Silas, I need help from those urges. I probably cannot otherwise keep a resolve to stick with Zayda. I look at a woman, feel drawn to her and to her secret places, and then I worry if she, too may have suckled at my mother's breast. You see, *radah* has aggravated the temptation all women represent; not only that: it has actually magnified my attraction to Melana, greatly so during your wedding time."

"You seek an excuse before you develop love? You seek a remedy more effective than resolution? How about my fists? Then, when you are quite thoroughly beaten, you will wish to hear my sermons, true?" came Silas's hot retort.

"I insist, Silas, a thrashing would not help; I have suffered dozens of beatings for my other offenses. Every man suspects my motives and clubs my deeds! I want more healing help or more effective resistance, Silas. Help me!" Caleb pleaded.

"Caleb, stop that whining! You sound like a cornered dog and must not always blame others for wrongs that you fashion in the forge of your mind. You have to look upward and make your own spiritual fortune. Have you considered prayer?" Silas probed, moved by persisting brotherliness.

"I pray seasonally, Silas."

"Dare I ask in what season? Every other summer?" Silas questioned, sharply. Then he asked, "Have you then pondered the message I bring, Caleb? The spiritual gift you may obtain simply by accepting it, eh? Are you disposed to provide a residence for the message of love, and honor it?" Silas reached for his own small jar, pouring out a modest helping of water for himself from Caleb's goat-skin vessel.

Seeming to take no note of Silas's action, Caleb looked down and then away as he replied: "I will say so, Silas. I will say so, but it is merely a desire, not a disposition —not this afternoon."

"Nonetheless, Caleb, kneel; now, Caleb, with so simple a token as these three drops of water, I do welcome you —much as the Pioneer John did, when Jeshua came to him for a blessing at BethAbara on the Jordan. I ask the blessings of the Holy Names: Creator, Child and Spirit for your soul. If you nourish it, it cannot escape. Now you are one of the new clan of believers and shall so remain if you will it. Welcome to the Way of Truth and Hope!"

Caleb pulled away, stood, and growled, "Abba, your friend Paul suggests that I do not need to do anything, except believe. You are saying I must nourish this conversion. Which is it?"

Silas spoke as the apostle he was. Silas, who —unlike his companion missionary —made no claims for himself, proclaimed his own view: "I am convinced that we must continuously renew the health of our souls; I hope those who read my epistle will find gentle guidelines for maintaining that necessary wellness which calls for both exercise and healing. If I stray in my behavior, I am not preserved for paradise unless I repent and mend my ways. Nor are you, Caleb, and I hold a responsible dissatisfaction for wrongs all others commit, hoping to work to overcome their effects."

"Effects?" Caleb queried.

"Yes, others may have been wronged," Silas reminded him, "and it will always be a good idea to try to repair the effects of those wrongs, which may include calluses on the spirit of the offender."

"Well, that's sure not the way Paul spoke when he dropped by last time," Caleb grumbled. "He said we don't have to do anything beyond belief, and also that we don't have to tell anyone that we are followers of the Way."

"Caleb, I am sure you don't credit that approach, even if you find it temptingly attractive. The Master charged us to spread the word and to show our belief by the form and color of our lives." Silas concluded by reaching for Caleb's hand, saying, "We should make a prayer."

They did recite some phrases, Silas praying aloud as he had been taught in temple. Caleb did not express his feelings boldly and only formed some words with his lips, words that Silas did not try to hear or decode. After a time, Silas said, "Caleb, you are in my prayers and have been incorporated among them since we first met. Now, let us again return to our homes; the shadows grow longer. I tire, but shall go back and tell this news. Melana will welcome it."

"All of it?"

"All, Caleb. And you, you may wish to start the habit of unending prayer. To answer all your questioners, you will need a good measure of guidance. We must now hurry along to be ready to attend to feeding the flock that awaits me at this evening's watch and singing. You will be—"

""Silas, I cannot. I have already made plans for this evening. I think Zayda, too…. Sorry."

Silas smiled at Caleb's excuse and let it go. "Another time, Caleb," he said. Caleb shrugged his shoulders.

As he hurried down Vermion's slope to the little house where Melana waited, Silas wondered, 'Will Caleb perhaps keep me in his prayers and thoughts?' Several aspects of that concern revolved in his mind as he approached their door.

When he told Melana what he had learned during the afternoon with Caleb, she was silent for a while. Then, quietly, she came to him; she looked at him strongly; she spoke with unmistakable meaning:

"*Radah*, eh? Silas, thank God, Caleb honored the tradition!"

AT THE VINEYARD, EARLY Inside these throbbing buds Hangs Truth's companion on the vine; Six months of noble exaltation Transforms the waters, sunshine, air and soul to diamond drops of wine.

CHAPTER 6.

VISIT FROM A WANDERER OUT OF TARSUS

/"Set your souls warmly aglow with prayer, that they may shine as lanterns on the mountainside, vanishing the darkness."— Epistle of Silas/

Dawn on a morning in late summer on the rivulet of the ThreeRivers, Tripotamos, which flows through Berea and borders Melana's garden. Wake-up prayers are completed, yet few from the deacon's mission have taken cooked food. A blurred sun breaks through the mists above the Vodas and Aliakmon Rivers.

Silas broils fish for the early meal. Pregnant Melana admires her vineyard, vines heavy with their purple-cluster fruit. She awaits Silas' call, wondering what new garnish he may add to the meal today. Sabaka, ever the alert watchdog, growls hoarsely; he runs barking from the front door, toward the gate. Melana, hearing the sounds of someone whistling, someone swinging up the path to the house, calls the dog back.

Silas also becomes aware of the visitation. 'Here comes a person of the spirit,' Silas thinks, remaining steadfast to his cooking. "Brother/Sister," he calls, "Who are you? Approach closer so we can see you."

When the man spoke, his Greek rumbled inside the well-padded consonants of Hebrew. Almost too indistinctly to be understood, he queried, "Why don't you try to guess who I am?"

Silas commanded, "Stay where you are! I want my wife to share in this action!" And the visitor halted his climb, staying just out of sight behind the thicket. Silas called Melana to insist that they must try to guess the identification of the stranger. "But you, Melana, not I, must guess. I would recognize this visitor's hide in a tanning vat!"

Melana shouted exploratory questions: "Are you from Athens? From Bithynia? Nabatea? Alexandria?" "No. No. No. NO!" came the pleased replies; then, "Shall I come closer, to give you a better inspection?"

"No, good friend, just turn your back to us," directed Silas.

When the bald man's back was turned, Melana called, "Then, are you Paul, out of Tarsus?"

With a great laugh, Paul rushed ahead, and Silas ran down the path to meet and welcome him. As hugs were exchanged and repeated, Paul growled at Melana, "How did you know me? You must be the miracle called Melana." And, touching her roundness, he asked "Second child?" She smiled and as she nodded, she caressed his hand on her belly.

"Well, Silas told me, told me by saying he would not permit himself to guess who you are. He knew, absolutely knew, so I knew, too!" she said as she reached down to pick up the dark-eyed Lydia-child. Going on, she added, "Yes, Paul, I am Melana and yes, I know you very well. You cannot hide in Macedonia. Come join us in our morning prayer and this nourishing meal of fish and fresh bread."

Paul did so after tying his donkey at the lower gate. Finishing, he hugged them all again, especially Lydia; then he said he must hurry, must go on to Thessalonica, to consult with Gaius and the others there.

(As Paul was leaving, Silas placed a fat wineskin in his pack. "This is for Gaius, Paul —our best wine, last year's. For Gaius, sorry ——not for you ——for Gaius.")

Silas and Melana worked through the remainder of the day, from time-to-time recalling and discussing Paul's works. "I hear," Melana said, "I hear that Paul has taken to preaching control of others' lives, especially women's lives. Is that so, and if it is, on what basis from the Master's teachings does he draw such an authority?"

"I have tried to bring him to a gentler approach, more in harmony with my learning, Melana", Silas replied. "Yes, he does take the position that women need to be instructed on every point of behavior, and he would have you and your sisters veiled to insure your modesty. I have to believe that a whore can have long hair, just as women of virtue can have tresses of any length. You may smile ——even laugh —also when I say that we men, too, have both saints and whores amongst ourselves." She did laugh, indeed, but asked, "Is it a man's gaze which Paul would shield against, or something more deeply set in humankind?"

FEASTING WITH THE DEACON

"I take it Paul would not only control you," said Silas. "I regret to add that he seems determined to make you invisible."

"Does he suppose that men must make noises and dress in colors but women's godliness is, in his mind, measured by hiding our beauty? Is that it, Silas?" Melana asked in some anger.

"None of us —men or women —are to gain by deceit," he replied, adding "Adornment is our addition to what God has given us in the mysterious make-up from our mothers' wombs —whatever that mystery holds." Silas concluded by reaching for her hand and whispering, "Beautiful Melana, with hair of spun midnight, I would not support any edict to cut your hair or to veil your face."

She smiled, squeezed his hand and kissed his cheek.

Just after dusk, a hard-breathing Caleb appeared at the door, carrying a deeply intoxicated Paul. Silas spoke: "I knew. I shoulder blame for this myself."

Caleb jumped into the awkward silence: "I came upon him as I was returning from Thessalonica. Your friend here was preaching your religion to a herd of goats.... There they stood, bleating at one another. Paul was whining about some 'thorn in the flesh' and caressing an empty wineskin. When he saw me and later spoke your name, I saw a chance to increase my treasury...." Looking slyly from Melana to Silas, he shot his dart at them: "With *radah* and this, I have a large account at this house, true? But I suppose it would be wrong to exploit the shortcomings of your friends, right, Silas?"

Melana commanded, "Caleb, take our forgiving love and your hauntings and go to your home."

Caleb left, and they put Paul to bed and prayed. Paul went on to Thessalonica the following morning after the three made a pact of peace that included a sample helping of Melana's recipe as an antagonist against one's appetite for wine: "It is made of burned bone." she said, adding that "I am told that it works, which we hope" and she pressed an embrace on the bright-eyed man from Tarsus.

"I am aware of the need to try it and shall do so, prayerfully, among friends," Paul promised.

It was many months before Silas constructed a patchy peace with Caleb, since Caleb did not favor the softening of their relationship, and Silas had held off asking for an explanation of the mention of *radah*. Melana, who seemed to know, simply collared him and brought him to the hearth where Silas prayed, and a form of truce took shape. Two seasons had passed since Caleb built his scheme for coercion. Love won a partial victory against the extortionist, who seemed to continue to harbor suspicions that led him to design some undercutting approaches against them, especially against Silas. However, tensions were temporarily lowered in that sector of Berea.

Later that season, the community absorbed the added love of a new baby boy at that little stone house, the house hidden by its garden behind the wide gate. Melana and Silas named the boy Joshua. Lydia called him 'Dosh.'

CHAPTER 7.

TROUBLE REVISITS

In the quiet of mornings, Silas increasingly counted the blessings of life. Now he had enjoyed seven years with Melana —eight in service to Berea, and the future appeared to offer a happy extension of times already called sacred.

"Seven treasured years!" he said aloud to Melana that morning shortly after the anniversary of their wedding day. Melana recited some of the achievements of those years: 'three little churches in Berea, two children, seven hundred souls worshiping in *agapae*.' "And more on special days," she added.

"My love," Silas proposed, "my goal is to enlarge the joys of all our days, in the years ahead. We will work most prayerfully to increase, above all, the number of worshipers."

Melana said, "I thought you were campaigning for increasing the number of worship houses nearby, my darling Silas."

In response, the deacon said, "Oh that would be good, but more precious would be, that is *will* be the increase of those who give thoughtful attention to the embrace of holy thoughts, regardless of the location or even if the house be a dungeon or a cave. I do not forget that I made a promise to myself to give my time and my days to that cause in Berea. Berea is my haven and my seat of action, as it seems to be for you, too.

Yes, Melana agreed, I want to remain here, laboring in Berea's gardens. I hope they continue to bear lovely fruit, she declared, looking squarely into the barefoot deacon's eyes. Although our plantings will not all show the rapid pace that we have realized during the past seven years.

These have been unusually rich harvests —seven fat years, should I say? observed Silas. I know we will meet some who accept the seed of the Word slowly others, somewhat slower still yet others, perhaps never perhaps there are some minds in which there is no medium for the cultivation of spiritual flowers.

As if to confirm the correctness of this view, a messenger from Caleb's house arrived at their door. Melana took the message. She and Silas read it together. Surprise! Caleb and Zayda want them to come for a meal today; just the two of them, for a special evening with the still unmarried couple.

"Perhaps they want our help in planning their wedding," Silas suggested, as if to hope it so.

"That would be our expectation, I know, but their long-delayed ceremony will astonish me if ever it occurs," Melana observed.

"Astonished I am," Silas replied, "that they have assembled a meal and planned to share it; they seem no more orderly than, than —"

"Than a gathering of believers from the Berean parokias, such as our crowd?" Melana inserted, completing his statement.

Silas agreed. They laughed and sang a fragment of a little song they had composed in very intimate privacy. Dancing, they laughed again, together....

Berea, village in the hills above the river spring, Enfold us; feed us while we dance; clap while the children sing;We dance to honor life and love, two gifts to us from God,And dance beneath the stars above —bare our heads, our feet unshod: Dance to glorify our God. We dance to honor God!

Overcome by their dual hilarity, they fell as a two-humped lump. "Oh, love, we will someday dance with such vigor that we shall throw the laces out of our sandals!" Melana promised. Recovering, they began making arrangements for the evening, first leaving Joshua and Lydia with Archos and his family, nearest neighbors. When they dressed, Melana got out her own petasos, an especially colorful head-piece for her black tresses.

"What a lovely hat!" Silas told her. "Let me get a closer look." She did, and they kissed, a soft and quiet kiss.

Down the hillside, Zayda got out her own colorful headpiece, which harmonized nicely with her reddish tresses. "You hardly call that a hat, do you?" Caleb snorted.

"No, Caleb, it is a collar for you to tug when you are jerking me into one of your plans!" Zayda snapped. "I wanted to look my best for your special lady, Melana, the TooGood wife of Deacon TooGood."

With a swift move, Caleb slapped hard at Zayda, knocking her combs out of her hair. However, she saved her face by out-racing his hand. As she glanced up the hillside, she pretended to see Silas, and she shouted, "They are almost here! I have to finish our meal, since you won't." Caleb then left off the chase and put away the slate on which he had been making notes.

Observing the bright sun of the late afternoon blazing down Mt. Vermion's valleys, Silas smiled; he turned and stared gently at his wife's head covering, reflecting that 'it symbolizes my further linkage to this woman, this Melana.' He and she had borrowed habits and customs, petasos and prayers, from Jerusalem, Alexandria and Athens. "What love!" he whispered to himself.

Taking a small container of sweets to share from the pantry, Melana bade their house a blessing from the gate and took her husband's hand. Off they hopped together, as lovers do. As lovers, they also went skipping up the weedy path to the house where they would be guests.

Zayda waited at the door and welcomed them with, "Caleb's companions drank our wine supply. They came back with us from Thessalonica and left very little food untouched and no wine." Continuing to complain, she whined, "You want to know what's unspent? Oh, they left my little container of dried peach leaves. I hope you like peach-leaf tea; seems a terrible drink to serve with roast lamb and squash.... You do like roast lamb, I guess? Not I—I do not care for it; for me, grouse. I made Caleb stew two grouse for me, Melana." "Sounds delicious!" Melana answered. "We do drink peach-leaf tea, thank you. Oh, Caleb, you have used rosemary from my herb garden, haven't you? The house smells so good! Sharpens our appetites, true, Silas?" The deacon winked responsively.

Everyone touched hands, and Silas moved toward the still sullen Zayda with a grin. "You will share a bite of the grouse with Deacon Silas, won't you?" She grudged him a smile and signaled for them to enter the dining area. As Melana brushed past her, she handed Zayda some candy sweets. "Lydia and I made these yesterday," she said; she sounded pleased. Zayda smiled a tight smile as she took the candies.

Caleb asked Silas to say a house blessing and, if he wished, to pray thanksgiving. The deacon nodded an acknowledgment, took off his petasos, and spoke a brief prayer that thanked the Infinite Provider.

Amens done, Silas joined Melana in thanking their hosts for the invitation. All four looked at one another in an uneasy wait for the dinner to begin. "What happened to your petasos?" Melana inquired, inspecting its torn edge.

"Caleb thinks it is a receptacle for dried figs and other debris," Zayda replied, "and it got the standard punishment for trash bins. Ri-i-i-i-ght, sweet Caleb?"

Caleb hissed. "We sometimes have the same problem," Melana said, smiling and touching Zayda's near hand, which Zayda withdrew on reflex. "Pray that it never happens again!" Caleb thundered.

Silas called upon his social skills to keep the chat flowing. "Oh, before I forget it," he said, "Melana and I want to thank the two of you for this invitation."

"When you leave, your appreciation will be greater or less," Caleb offered. With such ambivalence, Caleb had seldom come closer to Truth.

In the center of a small table, Zayda had placed a hard loaf. Next to the bread, a pitcher. Pointing to it, she identified as "our best peach tea." Four cups stood beside the tea pitcher, and Caleb offered to pour.

"With appreciation," Melana said, accepting hers, and, "To your health and good spirits," Silas offered, adding, "This is my first salute in peach-leaf tea!", which drew some amused smiles and half laughs. In the embarrassing silence that then followed, Zayda offered stools to her guests.

"Please sit, and while Caleb is finishing the meats, could I ask a question?" "Certainly, Zayda!" Melana replied, "If Silas cannot answer it, we shall find a good woman who can!"

"I am curious; Caleb says you speak of miracles and mysteries that make up your religion." She paused, staring hard into the deacon's eyes.

"Yes?" Silas inquired, adding, "Most of the time, I talk of the gifts of grace and faith; we do not over-dwell on other miracles. Life and the prospect of a joyful afterlife stand as quite miraculous to me, Zayda. What is your question?"

"Silas, how can bread and wine become the body and blood of a person long dead? Is that what you teach?"

"We do teach a very special remembrance of Jeshua, and we teach it in much the way you describe. We accept and believe that the Master is not dead, but that He died. A simple mystery."

Zayda and Caleb listened with exaggerated interest. Melana prayed silently. Silas simply continued: "We know that those who believe in that mystery, in the power of the Godhead as we do, they will find the substanc-

FEASTING WITH THE DEACON

es. In my own case, I do try to arrive at the celebration with correct intent and place the bread and wine in my hands caringly. In turn, the bread and wine rush to re-assemble into a supreme nobility. Truly so."

Closing his reply, Silas uttered his belief: "We cannot imagine anything else when bread and wind are transformed under such ceremonial devotion and circumstances of dedication."

"I shall fight to resist such an imagination," Zayda vowed.

"Your friend Paul, as I remember, has an even more zealous imagination," came from Caleb. "Paul searches for the meaning of life in wine flasks." Silas looked away, uttering a silent prayer for them all, especially favoring the absent man from Tarsus.

Caleb took a deep breath, slightly uneasy. Then, as if there had been no other intent, he announced the meal. He had been marking on the slate but left that off when he realized that the others' curiosity was making impossible the entry of secret, legible notes. So, "Fill your plates!" he suggested, "if you will be so kind." Melana asked for a moment so she might offer thanks and praise, and four people with two contrasting views on the matter joined hands as she voiced gratitude for a meal eaten largely in silence.

Unanimously, it was judged a deliciously filling meal. Silas said, "I especially enjoyed the sample taste of grouse which I thieved from Zayda's plate. She had indeed shared it, but scolded me, saying 'You certainly are greedy: lamb AND grouse!' Yes, you did, Zayda!" Caleb and Melana made faces at the deacon. It provided one of the rare moments of light-heartedness.

When they were finishing, Caleb admitted that he had invited them because he and Zayda had returned from Thessalonica only the day earlier, and he brought our his slate with a plan to propose. He cleared his throat and scratched his crotch ——both being actions of equal awkwardness and embarrassment. "Suppose," he said, "suppose I were to tell you that there is a request for a new overseer of your missions at Thessalonica? And that's not all: most of the people I know around here favor you to manage the eastern Macedonian region —you, to replace Gaius. No one wants Timothy back; everyone is afraid that Titus or some other Gentile will get the appointment, and the people with influence want the two of you to apply for the post, together!"

He paused, looking around the table, but no eyes met his. "Sound good?" he inquired. "I can arrange a meeting with the right people; just say the word."

Melana and Silas stood. Each knew the other's attitude about such an occupation, yet neither was truly surprized by Caleb's outrageous action. Zayda seemed to delight in Caleb's prospective scolding.

Silas' tongue found fire: "Caleb, stop your meddling! I will not accept the arrangement, and we do not desire the appointment. Please do not consider that you honor us, your busy neighbors, in this eviction by adding the balm of an opportunity for Melana. Neither she nor I would share ill-gotten rank. You surprise me again, Caleb! And, Zayda, if you acted in complicity with him in this intolerable and unrighteous plan, I must ask you to stop scheming to remove our influence from Berea, which we have come to love."

"It was just an idea, Silas," Caleb whined. "We thought you and the little woman would be grateful. Berea is just a mountain crossroads, a mere cluster of huts, compared with Thessalonica. Besides, the people who command the real power in that parokia have decided to push Gaius out. One of them told me Gaius is too fired up about devotionals and prayer services." Caleb said it: He and Zayda and their partisans could see the trophy. Certainly, if they were Silas and Melana, they would take it!

"Caleb," Silas said, lecturing him, "Caleb, Caleb! ... aah —we do honor Gaius for his zeal and his accomplishments. No one should reduce the self-respect that comes from recognizing one's own good works. We do so: Even forgetting the handicap of Gaius's crippled leg, we here and your friends in the big city owe him and the church freedom to continue his ministry. Any minor lapse —or, any major error —he may have allowed, it is no concern of yours, is it?"

Caleb stiffened his jaw muscles and made noises in his throat. Zayda rattled her tea cup and looked at the brim of the deacon's worn petasos.

Melana found her opportunity, as Silas paused. She spoke slowly, as she did for children in their starter lessons. Her manner and form of speech showed love for the stumbling ones, love laced with the reminder that they had done much injury. She addressed both of them: "Caleb, Zayda: We will do many things, but I must reject —I am confident Silas rejects —the offer you pretend to bring us. We will tend your gardens, hold your hand, pray for your increased happiness, and deliver the neighbors' babies. We will plead for remedies to relieve desperate causes —and yours appears so, if you do not take steps yourselves, to hold goodness close."

Taking strong offense, Zayda interjected, "Melana, we need no more of your scolding. We invited you here with good intentions, in the light of Caleb's fondness for you."

"Fondness? Oh?" Melana seized the term. "Call it a violation of *radah* and an insult to my marriage! We all recognize it as the seed of danger. I see that this danger of his disposition toward me, though uninvited, this danger persists. Yet, even in my desire to avoid it, I do not propose that Silas and I uproot ourselves from our mission in Berea to install the two of us as replacements for Gaius, an old friend."

"And," Silas tacked on, "and leaving our healing and teaching ministry behind to become keepers of records in charge of a cage of documents. We would become prisoners of ledgers, as your father was in Alexandria, Caleb. He chose to be an accountant. Very well, but I could not choose the counting-house trade; my calling is otherwise."

"Silas, you are an idiot if you expect to escape such duties," Caleb remarked. "After all, your precious church, which brings you such pride —it will need overseers and treasurers."

"Yes," the deacon acknowledged, "and indeed, Caleb, we can hope that there are more monies than the missions here have received. Levying and collecting are not for us, however; nor are tallying and record-keeping. Moreover, I hope the church's future treasury officials do not paint themselves generals. We need shepherds; caring shepherds —caretakers and healers, as I had hoped you would become, Caleb: Shepherds to teach the ways of the Chief Shepherd, caring for and loving the lost and maimed."

Melana spoke, with extreme gentleness. "Sometimes we regard you as the lost and —"

"And maimed?" Zayda challenged. "If you only knew how we have suffered!"

"But the spiritual suffering we see in this home, Zayda, it seems in balance," Silas ventured.

"Oh?!" she blazed.

"Yes," he dared further, "although the Compassionate Master does not so shape it, the pain in your souls seems quite proportionate with the degree you admit falling short of doing right and justly for others."

"That is donkey manure and most unfair, Silas! You are not welcome at this hearth if you believe that," Caleb flared, "and you will please go."

Silas had already retrieved his petasos, which he placed at a smart angle, high above his forehead. He started toward the door.

"Yes, we are leaving," Melana agreed; "but, as we depart, I ask that you think deeply about the penalties you have paid and will pay again in life. They usually match the quality of wrongs we inflict. If so, accept the penalties. That match of wrongs and penalties may offer you a way to render justice."

Zayda stared at Melana and Silas, eyes of anger, hands forming fists. She stormed, "I do not intend to offer justice!"

Melana, standing now at the door, turned with a final word, a promise: "Look at it in this way: The ills you might suffer for doing good, those can be the jewels of your crown, your true rewards. Search for them, and take this hug from me, Zayda."

But Zayda turned sharply away, and Silas captured the embrace his wife had extended to Zayda at the doorstep. "Zayda," Silas cautioned sharply, "I shall plant no seeds in frozen soil; you would offer only a chilled and barren space for the seeds of the Way of the Redeemer. It is best, then, to hold off serving those great goods or until your soul thaws."

In an awkward move, Caleb pushed his groin toward Melana, pushed at Zayda, and made his routine obscenity move toward Silas, shouting, "You —both of you, will regret turning down this last chance to profit from our friendship and our generous offers!"

Silas and Melana returned to their own home in near silence. On the hillside behind God's thicket, they prayed quietly and generated love.

Back in his house with Zayda, Caleb slammed the door, cursing at her. "You really cost us the best chance we had of —"

"Of getting Melana's mind, so that you could at last capture her body? Was that it; was that the idea, Caleb?" Zayda accused.

"Not so! For months now," Caleb inserted, "since I first decided that the mysteries of the Way were silly myths, I have been considering an alternative to the gentle and apparently-forgiving manner of men such as Silas.

"There is an alternative to combat it, there really is, Zayda. Sit down and listen. You recall the rebels of discord told of by the lore of our forefathers? Do you? They were the so-called Sons of Shuthelah, the first Shuthalhites. Now, I think it is time for me to lead a movement against the Way, as modeled on the notorious Christ of Nazareth."

"Oo-ooh! You scoundrel and low-life! I love it!" Zayda squealed, hugging Caleb and performing a hot dance for him. "Oh yes, what can we do to put down that mission of Silas and Melana?"

FEASTING WITH THE DEACON

"I am not sure I want your help, woman," Caleb replied, cowering from the blow that Zayda shaped and delivered with her kick. "I shall ignore that injury because I may ask you to take on some duties of my new organization, having been today inspired to proceed with setting up the Neo-Shuthalhites, here or in Thessalonica. Won't that be great? The new Rebels of Discord. Who will compose our songs and anthems?"

"Zayda, find some disgruntled member of Silas's mission temples and bribe him in any way to get us started. Tell him we are using the book of Numbers —the fourth Book of the Pentateuch —as our model."

"And, dear Caleb, my stud Rebel, did you not say that I am to use any way, any approach, to lure that inspiring composer?" Zayda tried to capture the idea, but she itched too much to keep it between her ears. Still, she would be a campaigner for him for awhile, with such zeal: "Oh this will be a picnic of scandal! What an opportunity for making a contribution. I am getting started directly. Now."

CHAPTER 8.

CEPHAS CALLS A SCRIBE TO ROME

\"God grants no evil ends."—Epistle of Silas/

***

Archos, who had finally purchased the tavern, came early to the doorway. Melana greeted him smiling, inviting him: "Silas has just made breakfast; join us!" Archos accepted the invitation: "Praise God for this house!" he said loudly, entering.

Silas turned, nodded, and teased his wife and his caller by addressing Lydia. "If your mother wishes to distribute my cooking to the elect of Berea, why not invite Caleb?" Lydia added a nod of her chin to her smile and skipped off. She knew the way to most of the family's acquaintances, Silas mused as he watched her disappear on her errand. "Oh, that precious child, so bright!—she and her brother and little sister. Archos! Have you seen our baby? Here, Joshua: show him your new sister."

"Papa, Johara is almost a year old!" Joshua replied, in a tone of impatience for Silas. The Deacon shrugged and all of them laughed, including the baby Johara, whom her proud brother lifted as high as he could.

"Such spirited gifts for parents all three of you Children," Archos observed.

Melana looked up, smiling; Silas touched Archos's hand, agreeing, then he asked, "What really brought you to this happy house? What, in addition to the flavors and fragrances that my newly baked bread lend the morning air?"

"This" Archos offered, "This message, which was left at the tavern; a courier left it late last night " —but Archos was interrupted by Caleb's call from the doorway, acknowledging the beckoning from Lydia, as he shouted, "If you dispatch such charming agents with all your calls, Deacon, I would hearken to your invitation every morning!"

Silas looked up; "We shall carefully keep that in mind, Brother Caleb. Thank you for coming today. Yes, we assumed a pretty, young woman could convince your to come for a tasty meal. Caleb, Archos has just delivered a written message —Oh,I do see it is from John at Ephesus. He brought this message as well as his appetite for a share of the bread, cheese and figs."

Caleb asked, "Does the message suggest going to Ephesus or bring news of Jerusalem, or —perhaps —Rome?"

Lydia jumped into the inquiry; with an unmistakably wise smile, Silas' brown-eyed daughter affirmed Caleb's implied claim on her father. "Will it mean that you will have to travel?" she worried. Silas had raced through the scrawl that characterized Bishop John's hand and could reply, "Yes, Rome," he asserted, "but let us come near together. I shall read it aloud, and we can all hear what he has written. Then we can try to factor its meaning while we enjoy this food from God's bounty."

Everyone became quiet as Silas read the brief note: "Greetings —Join me in 20 days in Corinth for a reunion and a review of news from Rome.

In the Name of the Prince of Johara is almost a year old!" Joshua replied, as if impatient with his father. Silas shrugged and all of them laughed, including the baby sister, whom Joshua, her proud brother, lifted as high as he could.

"Such spirited gifts for their parents," Archos observed.

Melana looked up; Silas held Archos's hand, agreeing, then asked, "What brings you here? What, in addition to the flavors and fragrances my newly baked breads lend the morning air?"

"This," Archos offered. "This message. It was left at the tavern by a courier last night—"

But Archos was now interrupted by Caleb's call from the doorway: "If you dispatch such charming agents with all of your calls, Silas, I would listen for your invitation every morning!"

Silas looked up. "We shall carefully keep that in mind, Brother Caleb. Thank you for coming today; we assumed a pretty young woman could convince you to come for a tasty meal.... Caleb, Archos has delivered a written message —oh, I see it is from John at Ephesus —brought a message as well as his appetite Shepherds."

FEASTING WITH THE DEACON

Silas reported, "It is signed: John, Overseer at Ephesus." Its date showed it had been written eight days earlier. Melana and Silas knew that some of the authorities' pressures on the other leaders had threatened the survival of the church; if John the Beloved considered a meeting necessary, Silas would go to the 'reunion' in Corinth. He packed for a fortnight, hugged his family for an hour, agreed that Melana could handle prayer and healing services, and tied his new black petasos under his chin. Down the path to the boat landing at Pydna he headed, singing.

The warm winds of March had begun to visit Berea when he returned from the meeting at Corinth, and Melana had planted several of her garden crops. Silas rushed to visit her in the garden as soon as he arrived back on the Vermion slopes. "What tasks did you discuss; will you have to go traveling again?" she asked, pulling last year's dry weed stalks from the path of the furrow for this year's squash. "Has Nero named his scapegoats for last year's fire in Rome?"

"Yes, love, as I first guessed; there are concerns for Jews and also for both Paul and Peter as well as their congregations. Peter has asked for me to assist him in preparing a letter to the mission flock. As I may have told you, Peter has never learned to read or write.... You'll recall that I served as his co-author and scribe out of Antioch years ago."

"So, he needs you again, Silas?" she asked, using a stick to make a love sign in the earth.

Silas smiled at the symbolic marking, and nodded, adding, "Yes, my darling, but it goes beyond simply providing literacy. John, our holy brother, has had a visitation, a vision that reveals Peter's fear of death at the hands of the Emperor's minions: Peter thinks he will likely be executed at some forthcoming festival."

"Perhaps he is merely tired or ill. It would not seem unnatural to me to find him possessed by fears, given the circumstances," offered Melana, "although I don't mean that you should change plans. Go to Rome and help him do what he wants to do."

"Naturally," said Silas, "Peter wants to leave a record of his own beliefs and devotions for future generations. He would want to discuss his writings —not merely dictate them to some Roman hireling who may be both uninspired and unqualified to enter a discourse with Peter."

"What about Paul?" interrupted Lydia, who had gathered with some of the other Bereans to welcome her father but had not had a moment to recognize his return. Now was he off again? She and two others gave him forceful hugs, and he paused to return their embraces before answering. But she seemed somewhat alarmed that Silas was not staying in Berea. "Must you always be on departure? Is Paul doing his part in this?"

"Paul is not at Rome, Lydia," Silas said. "He is traveling. He continues to compete with the Caesars in exploring the West, especially Tarshish, or as we now call it, Iberia, named by the Romans, Hispania.

"Come close, Lydia, and listen: With the assistance of many others, including yourself, your mother and I conduct an intensive mission whose center is Berea. However, much remains to be done in this mission, and I hope that you will want to continue it."

"I realize that you regard it as important work. Why, then, can't you stay here and do it? Is Paul so precious that his list of 'Things to Do' outranks other missioners' lists?" Lydia pressed on with her questions.

Silas seemed to want to explain, instead of debating his daughter. However, he felt the power of her suasion and reported somewhat lamely, "Paul moves along rapidly as if he were engaged in a lightning war of evangelism against Evil. Our friend from Tarsus draws his mission as broad as the expanding Empire, but I agree, I am concerned about his apparent failure to embrace and nourish his converts. He has taken organized conquest as a command, with the rules of the conquest written by himself." Silas seemed somewhat exasperated, and his daughter realized that Silas was on her side of the debate. Her mother, too

Melana's brow wrinkled. "I wonder if he can sustain this effort aiming for Charity: love with a missionary community."

"Dearest, you express that question as wonderment, but I would worry if he were to have such a community —such an army," Silas admitted.

"But Paul's zeal, his fire for the Word, runs at a pretty steady beat, doesn't it?" Melana asked for confirmation.

"True, my treasure; it is all for the glory of God, I know," Silas replied, adding, "His steady servant who met us in Corinth said Paul is currently traveling among the mountains in Northern Iberia with plans to cross those mountains into Gaul. Ambitious, yes: The servant told us in Corinth that Paul anticipates future journeys into Caesar's islands far to the north, where the Britons live.

"So, we can anticipate the spreading circle, running the message out with no loss of strength. As we know that is contrary to the way circles in

FEASTING WITH THE DEACON

water weaken as they widen.... A miracle, that preservation of strength.... We can marvel at the effect of Words broadcast without swords. As here," Silas continued, "curious new believers step forward from their tribe, sometimes abandoning their people."

Melana said, "It is really astonishing, that way of allowing their curiosity free rein when every member of their own tribe relies belligerently on belief in false gods, gods presumed vengeful."

"Someday," observed Silas, "I suppose, the missioners' humanity will get in the way and the unity of the growing community may break down, but I pray for the spread of this glorious Oneness."

"Amen! praise God in His mysteries," Melana added; Lydia and now Joshua drew into their parents' embrace. All four of them felt a strengthening of faith that Silas shared with the same childish awe shown by Joshua and Lydia.

The quiet moment of worship gave way to the noise of Caleb's stampeding rush along the path to the garden; he appeared out of breath, his spirit astir. "Caleb, you should not try to run uphill; that is for young people!" Melana teased.

He ignored her. "Silas," Caleb pushed further, saying, "I hear that you may be leaving for an extended trip —to Rome, I suppose?" "Yes, and do you wish to go, also? Or, as happily, to finish the little mission house you promised for Emathia, while I am away?"

"Awwh! Do not poke at me, Silas. I am in trouble and want your advice before you depart again."

"Trouble? Caleb, let us go to the little space we have set aside for prayer, so you and I can deal with it privately, not placing a burden on you or my family, agreed?" Melana and the children acknowledged the arrangement, and Melana led them back to the house above the Tripotamos to begin preparing for Silas' trip to Rome.

When they were alone in the secluded clearing, Caleb growled, "It is Zayda, Silas; she threatens to leave me unless we marry."

"Caleb, did you not promise me, years ago, to resolve or wrap up your association with Zayda?"

"Yes, Deacon, I recall. But I expected she would adopt a holy and moral life, and she remains unconverted and unacceptable, adding to my troubles."

"Oh? And you? Caleb, have you really accepted the gift I have described? Have you adopted the Way open to you?" Walking away, Silas finished, "Until you radiate the joy, voice the praise, and pray the petitions that visit my life, I will ask you to save your troubles in a big black bag.... When I return from Rome, welcome me back more nobly clothed, Caleb. I shall pray for you daily; mend your ways, with the help of Berea's spiritual community, your neighbors. Farewell, now."

Caleb felt satisfied that he had stirred things up a bit and told himself: 'We may be slow in building up a membership in the Rebels of Discord, but we are getting there, little by little.' And he checked again the distance from his cottage to the house where Melana and her children would be sleeping, unprotected, in the weeks ahead during Silas's absence....

For his journey across western Greece, Epirus and Dalmatia, Silas asked for the companionship of Mauros, now a member of the daughter church in Edhessa. A well-digger from western Macedonia, Mauros had volunteered earlier: "Deacon, if you ever need a strong companion or assistant, let me be that person." Under the circumstances, but mostly because of his familiarity with the difficult passage to the Dalmatian coast, Mauros was the outstandingly logical choice. Melana observed, "Silas, I will be relieved to know you have a strong companion, so expert in the ways of Nature and spirited in his belief, as Mauros is."

"Yes, and I am relieved to recall you have the good strong dog, Sabaka. Someday, when life permits as much contemplation as vigilance, I hope we may bring a kitten into the house."

Joshua and Lydia clapped and squealed, "Papa, do get us a kitten. Mother, may we have a kitten?" And smiles of that anticipation shared the farewells that early morning as the Deacon headed for Rome and a commission from Cephas. Just as he disappeared down the hillside path, Melana shouted for him to stop, and she ran to give him a spousal hug. Pulling Silas aside for a farewell embrace, she took a small locket from her robe, telling him, "I have an old friend in Dyrrachium: Heldaiah, who operates the large grist mill at the docks. Find her, dearest, and give this to her. Then arrange to stop at her place of business or her lodgings on your return trip."

North to Edhessa and coursing westerly along the Via Egnatia, toward Dyrrachium they go. Clouds of the forthcoming winter loom to the North, borne on boreal winds and making a grayish white backdrop for

FEASTING WITH THE DEACON

Dalmatia's great port. Still, it is warm enough for wild flowers, and Silas stops often to admire them. "Look, Mauros!" he calls on finding clovers and taking note of the bees among them. "Mauros, see the honey in formation? In intent, may I say, these clovers and those bees combine to become our future honey.

"Let us do a spiritual toast to those sweet workers: *Ut Apes!* To the bees, who produce honey for our appetite's delight."

"Or for the local bears, Deacon," Mauros replies. "Bears, they take even more spirited delight than I in raiding honey hives, but it is quite a mystery of nature that provides us such a sweet offering."

The next day they find themselves in Dyrrachium itself. Near the temple they find Titus, another of the Thessalonian brothers. He insists that Silas roast the lamb, just slaughtered, for a feasting, although Silas says, "I had expected some delicious fish from the Ionian. Or, perhaps lobster; did you not have fresh lobster today?" Titus shrugs, and Silas accedes to reality by calling for the local herbs, especially mint, to flavor the lamb, which the entire household enjoys. After dinner, Titus and Silas briefly discuss the progress of their mission works and those of Luke, Titus' brother, who brings Matthias, a local supporter. Some mention is made of the differences among the approaches of the chief missionaries —some flattering to Silas, some critical.

Matthias reports to Silas on the name 'Heldaiah,' the name of Melana's friend. "Heldaiah is a name only rarely found among women in western Macedonia, Silas, and I think it belongs to the Hebrew families from Alexandria, possibly Thessalonica." He tells Silas, "If she is in Dyrrachium, I am sure that I can find her —your Melana claiming that she operates a mill —but I will need more time to hunt for her; the grist mill by the docks is not in the most genteel area of the city, you know."

Silas nods understandingly. "Thanks to both you and Titus for trying. Perhaps, when I return from Rome.... But now, let us enjoy the evening and our meal."

Foods are offered; more prayers are said together with more sweets, including the dates and figs Mauros and Silas have brought. There are stories and a period of drinking, dancing and singing. The drinking is moderate, not incorporating so much wine that anyone approaches *methismenos*, fully drunk, but the entire group feels the pleasant sting of the grape. Titus says, "We are not *stoupi*, right?" but the dancing continues until the publican rings his bell and begins to snuff candles. So, finally, Silas urges an end to the sweets, saying, "We should leave some appetite on our plates, eh? But, we may glory all night!"

"Good night, Silas!" comes from Titus and the others.

Some of the small party may have gloried all night, as Silas had suggested. He slept well and woke with a new thought about Melana's friend, Heldaiah. He asked Matthias to help find a messenger who would take a paid commission to Berea and find Melana to ask for help in identifying Heldaiah, who must have known Melana in Alexandria. Even before the daybreak meal fed them, Mathias had located just such a traveling messenger who was on his way to Athens and would stop to do that simple favor in Berea for a few coins. So, Silas hastily wrote the necessary note and paid the messenger in a mixture of coins that seemed appropriate. Then Mauros and Silas were ready to go to the massive docks at Dyrrachium, and to go on to meet Simon Peter, whom he had also once known as Cephas.

By boat, they traveled across the Ionian straits to a harbor on the Calabrian heel of Italy; by foot and donkey across to Antium and on north to Rome three days later....

Mauros, who had begun an inquiry en route to Dyrrachium, continued to engage Silas in lengthy discussions of the beliefs they had previously held and those they now held. Mauros insisted on asking about the end of time and the eternity of paradise. Silas paused to say that he did not know all the details of the afterlife, but, "I take it to be *Eyn Sof*, that is without end."

They spent a major part of the time for the long journey to Rome looking at various sides to morality and responsibilities, broadened to include matters beyond shunning wrongs. Urged by Mauros, Silas suggested means to display charity toward the sick, needy, and those without shelter. In that regard, Mauros admitted that he had "not considered the welfare of others as any concern of mine until I began to give thought to power of love and the need to share it." Silas considered that admission a good sign. "As we draw nearer to Babylon, I find both of us getting closer to the central themes of the Way," he said.

Thus, on exhausted donkeys, Mauros and Silas entered Rome and arrived at the appointed place to meet Peter and Paul. According to Peter, Paul had returned only the previous day from a journey to Caesaraugusta on the Iberos River in Northeastern Spain. Over a dessert of Peter's

FEASTING WITH THE DEACON

sweetbreads, Paul confessed, "Yes, Silas, I overextended myself and the church.... We have to consolidate our work; we must tend the flock we have already begotten."

"Yes, Paul; Peter and I have tried to remind you that men and women require their spiritual remedies in doses over time; I have, in fact, come here to help seal up some small leaks that have developed in Peter's churches in Asia. I hope you will keep aware of the difficulty created when those who tend the vineyard at Thessalonica find the vines tangled by a great wind, blowing on Iberian settings or elsewhere."

"You do have a marvelous way of urging me to think farther ahead, Silas."

"Paul, I want to add one suggestion, now that I have captured your ear: Please stop trying to set everything into codes and commandments; my Greeks do not accept the Way as a reference to calibrate their conduct, and I doubt we can create an army of believers who spy on one another to report violations."

"Silas, you are too tolerant, as I observed in Corinth. If you allow flexible faith, you invite private interpretations and the end of our crusade. I must prescribe the ways for a believer and will persist in this to the end, which comes near."

"We will always differ on this, Paul; I will teach the Truth, provide the best foods possible to my guests, and catalog the miracles for them." Paul tried to interrupt, but Silas plowed ahead with, "Also, I shall tell jokes on Jesus' time and allow my congregations suppleness in their behavior. I want to go to Heaven relaxed and laughing," Silas concluded, smiling.

"Good night, Silas. Peter and you and I will have to deal with our differences again. Pray on it."   "I never cease. Good night, Saul —er-errh, Paul."

***

\"Pray, but keep in mind that God is not a servant."—Epistle of Silas/

CHAPTER 9.

COMPOSING THE EPISTLE OF PETER

\"We should not strain on trifles or choke on fine-choppings of the law when we offer God praises."—Epistle of Silas/

✳✳✳

As dawn broke over Rome, Silas came awake with a vision of good deeds that cried out for attention by followers of the Way. On his second day in the Imperial City, he foresaw additional missions, goals that he must address. Jumping from his cot and ignoring the breakfast Julia had set at his doorway, he called Peter and Peter's household together to discuss a need and a plan based on his observations that there were many in the city who did not have food or shelter.

"I do not notice many Romans who appear to care about providing for those hungry homeless," declared the deacon. "We must practice our charity. In fact, I believe the army of charitable followers of the Way should outnumber our army of cloistered mystics. Let us start such an army. We could, perhaps, make its headquarters here at your house, Peter...?"

Peter found this proposal strongly to his liking, and he walked to the doorway of his home, calling on Julia to "keep the door open, provide decorations leading on into the kitchen for their meals, and still onward to the sleeping quarters, for those who need a place to sleep."

Paul frowned, saying, "You will spend so much of your strength on running your inn that you will have no time to pray. Besides, I have been informed that the Emperor has instructed the chief magistrates of Rome to require strict enforcement of all laws and ordinances, including laws against foreign cults operating commercial enterprises."

"Well," Silas offered, "this would not be a commercial enterprise, to use your term. As for time to pray, I do that with every breath, without ceasing, anyway. This house, Peter's house, would have an open gate, with no fees and no charges —just as Melana and I offer Bereans. Faith and Love will be the only fees for joining, and even they will not be required, right, Peter?"

"I fear that your undertaking will be bankrupt on all accounts before the month is ended," Paul argued, "but let it go, if Peter is in favor."

And Peter stood beside Silas, announcing, "I am indeed, in favor."

That issue settled, they turned to Peter's 'heritage' letter, attending to it for the remainder of the day, except to lay in a supply of foodstuffs for those who might be knocking at the door during the night.

Silas got up four times to prepare late-night meals for those who called, but he took delight in the task. He seemed to find restoration there, reviving from the task itself, such that he did not appear to need the sleep that would normally have pulled at his eyelids. Mauros noticed that. So did Peter, who came into the dining quarters just before dawn, and just before he went back to bed.

Peter asked "Silas, How are things coming along,?" He accepted a smile from Silas, who said, "We are all enjoying this, Peter, and I have tried to provision your larder well enough to enable you to give them the best soups, stews, and sweets in the week ahead. I am confident that you and I believe we should not serve these, the poorest of Rome, not with the poorest of our leftovers. Serve them the best we can give, and share lovingly." Peter applauded, as did Mauros and the walls in all the rooms of the house.

To harmonize with the plan to share, as well as to fit Peter's larder, Silas conscripted Julia, Mauros and Peter to work with him to prepare a stock of braised vegetables: turnips, carrots, onions and peppery spices. "This dish," said the Berean deacon, "this recipe accommodates continuous sampling and replenishment. It calls for chopping the vegetables and adding water to sustain the pot, as well as periodically adding chives, peppercorns, thyme, parsley and vinegar. Cook the vegetables, but try not to overcook them, and consider toasting some almonds to toss into each serving.

"Julia, I am going to leave you in charge of this work and am going to bed, knowing it is in good hands." Julia and Mauros joined Peter in saluting Silas' exit with a short hug.

On the third morning of his stay in Rome, Silas awoke to a day that was to put the finish on Peter's letter to his 'scattered ones.'

FEASTING WITH THE DEACON

In coming awake, Silas realized how much he missed the children and Melana. Mixed with his meditation and prayers came a flood of memories, longing for her face, to touch and hold her so close he melted into her, all the boundaries of their territorial maps dissolving —she and Silas becoming one. Shameless in their dream-like ecstasy, he migrated into his love for her, and Melana seemed to materialize as he awoke. Who would dare dispute their intimacy? Dawn sent reveries and sleepiness away, and Silas walked to the room Julia and the missioners had reserved for writing, eating, visiting and debating. All functions would go to test today, testing in Berea as well as Babylon.

Meanwhile, the messenger found in Dyrrachium approaches Berea via Edhessa, enters the village, and makes inquiries about Melana. He questions a man standing by a roadside taverna, and the man (who is Caleb), who identifies himself as a close friend of Melana, offers to 'take care' of the message, sending the messenger on down the road to Thessalonica. determine what message Silas has sent. On discovery, Caleb resolves to dispatch Tamara, one of his former associates, to Dyrrachium. He coaches her in 'Silas lore' and instructs her carefully to displace Heldaiah and to substitute herself, arranging for her to make contact with Matthias, who does not know Heldaiah, and to sequester herself near the docks, pending Silas's return from Rome.

Peter, today, had undertaken the morning meal. Silas took advantage of the consideration to waken more fully, standing in the doorway. But the odors from the fireplace suggested some unusual culinary skills at play, but not until he walked toward his host did he observe the sufferings borne by Peter's breakfast makings: Peter had scorched the bread, boiled the kettle dry and spilled the washed fruits across the dirty floor. "Well, Silas, it appears that I am all thumbs today!" he admitted, looking up.

Silas chuckled, recalling the meals they had enjoyed together in Antioch. "Cephas," he cautioned, "all of your friends speak kindly of the big fisherman's thumbs. We should proceed with blessings and breakfast, I suggest, to take advantage of our early rising."

Peter voiced a simple grace-for-meals and motioned Silas to begin eating: "Yes, Silvanus, you said we would complete the letter today; I have arranged for a servant scribe to work with us."

"Oh, I have skills for all that a scribe would do. What will he provide for us?" Silas asked, somewhat annoyed.

"Not he... she, Silas," Peter replied with a wide grin. "Not all of Rome is male, Silas! Julia has worked with us before, and she is not only a follower of the Way, but also quite apt; not only apt, but also attractive; not only attractive, but also connected to some influence here in the capital."

"Outstanding! You and Paul will need another virtuoso after I leave!" Continuing with his light punches, Silas asked, "And can she cook?"

Peter, not renowned for his humor, said he did not know about her other talents. Silas withdrew from making unrelated remarks and began to study the writings that lay strewn about the work table. Stiffening, he re-examined those he had carefully copied from Peter's sayings the previous evening. He snorted. He set the manuscript papers aside and confronted Peter: "Friend, did you and Paul find fault with the writings that were so prayerfully developed yesterday? And, if that is true, why did you not consult me before allowing your letter to take on a tone you had never proposed?"

"Tell me what you mean, Silas."

Silas picked up the scroll sheets that reflected the past two days' labors, and began, "Here, Peter, we had *'By reason of your good works, glorify God when you receive grace, for it is the will of God that your well doing may correct the ignorance of free-seeking servants of God. Honor all...'*

"Now —NOW! —it reads: *'The Gentiles, by reason of your good works, may glorify God when they receive grace. Submit yourselves to every humans ordinance, whether to kings of to their governors sent for vengeance. For it is the will of God....'*

"And then, it goes on, Peter, several times sprinkled with the hard phrases of a military officer or jailer. The intent of the letter is changed. It no longer reaches out in charity. As it now stands, it directs and admonishes the hearer to obey all controls and commands; it has become the epistle of Paul and Peter Is it not time to accept that Paul has run through his inspiration, time to permit you to assert your own?"

"Silas, you know me —I cannot debate one so skilled; but I know that you and Paul and I partake of the same goodness. We ought to talk about our differences, and that means including Paul in our discussions since he authored the passages that offend you. I shall call him; he spent last night in the vacant house next door."

Silas re-read the phrasings that he found so worrisome. They comprised a string of admonitions to slaves and spouses that implied approval to any knave who elected to dominate and oppress others. This counsel strayed far from the exhortations to charity Peter had voiced only yesterday.

Now, at the door, here they were, the two of them: Paul and Peter.

"Silas, Peter tells me you claim I say we have a religion of rebels who should be pushed down," Paul said in the tone of an offended commander. "What is it that would please you: a hybrid text of Paul, Peter and Silas? That would be a weak and weaseled approach, the product of sick cats!" he stormed.

Silas stood his ground: "I want to assert that we do not have a religion of sick civet cats, Paul. More importantly, and unlike you, I have not tried to put my twist on Peter's words. Rather, this morning I want to restore his words as he authored them yesterday and earlier. I do not want to produce the Epistle of Silas and Peter, but to be a helpful scribe for Peter. That is all."

"No, Silas," Peter inserted, "I mean, yes, Silas: Go right ahead and tell Paul what bothers you; that is a way for the three of us to find peace and for the two of you to guide me to the final form of my epistle."

"Very well," Silas continued, "Paul, I hope we can agree that we are to strive for perfection, to walk the Way in the example given by the life of the Master."

Paul nodded. "And remember, Silas, I have already given them a perfect model of the expected conduct, directing them to obey the officers who enforce the model."

"Two new problems appear, friend. First," Silas enumerated, "enforcers are no more illuminated than those who would submit, and second, our congregations have only begun to develop spiritual endurance from the strengths so recently given them. I fear you treat them as weaklings and display the church as a prison, or at best, a refuge."

"Silas, a refuge is just what most of them require. They are stupid! Most of their acts are futile, especially those of their women."

"My, my! How our personal outlook does influence the formulas we shape for others! I see imperfections, too, but not limited to women," Silas countered. "I approach it with a zeal that calls for all of us to work to help one another in our striving for the good and the true."

Now Paul jumped on a flaw he found in Silas' approach. "Deacon, most of our friends do not worship in such constancy, such fervor, such hope for correctness as you think. We have to remind them of all that is required of them, give them rules to follow, and then honor them with little tokens and bouquets that celebrate their obedience."

Cephas reminded the two debating disciples,"I appreciate what you two friends are trying to do. I also see some of the problem between you, Paul, and Silas —who worries about putting too many restrictions and not enough lovely ceremonies into place around moral situations. Paul, I do wonder about the prospect of a religion with so many details that it draws a new body of law into being, just when we have been freed from such by the Master, our Redeemer."

Paul tried again: "Peter, you will require a set of rules, more than a framework, a reference, a calibration for people. Most members of your congregation are weaklings who do not understand the mysteries."

Silas inquired, "Do you and I? I think not. Also, I do not agree that our congregations represent unthinking weaklings. If they may indeed rely on spiritual crutches when they make first inquiries, they mature and strengthen as they invest themselves in prayer and study. Thus, they differ none from you and me in their humanity and their wonder at miracles and mysteries."

Peter laughed. "There we have it, I think. Please recall, both of you, that I am the only one of the three of us who accompanied the Master and listened to him day after day. Since I am to contemplate signing off as the author of the epistle Silvanus/Silas has agreed to carry back to Berea and Thessalonica, I am again taking charge of its words and ideas. I can do that because I am the biggest man in the room! To accomplish it, I shall think it over all by myself for a while; then, I shall rejoin you, Silvanus, to ask you to complete the writing when Julia has sketched it out for me in its new form."

Peter's proposal being urged on them in that way, Paul and Silas embraced and prayed together, exchanging bits of news while they waited for Julia to bring back the newly enscribed epistle from Peter. She had also prepared a small noon-day meal that all four of them could share lovingly while they contemplated Peter's work.

"Cephas," Silas called out to Peter after he and Paul had gone over the text, "Cephas, Petros, RockyStone, whatever solid name you accept, SimonPeter: These words have established solid footing again. Good, Peter, but you still have not restored a consistency with what you said yesterday

FEASTING WITH THE DEACON

or with my accommodating form of the Way.... O-oh-ooh! Paul whispers that he still sees too much accommodating pliancy and freedom made available by your teaching; so, the three of us will depart from this session taking somewhat different spiritual paths. I think that is good; it fits what the Berean experience has taught me." Smiling at Julia, he added, "It also fits what I admire in both of you that you should have recruited Julia—such a capable scribe with notable skills in cooking, too!" Julia smiled, touching Silas on the shoulder as she passed a glass of grape juice to him.

"Enough, enough!" Paul shouted, laughing. "Finish it, and let us send this good man back to Berea. Before I forget, let me send my appreciation to Melana for the bone meal recipe. It helped greatly in the struggle against my unruly appetite for drink."

"She will be pleased to hear of your victory over a bad habit, Paul," agreed Silas. "Even more, she will praise the news of the shelter kitchen that Peter and Julia are setting up for the poorest of Rome."

All three of the striving missioners smiled and embraced: Peter, Paul and Silas. Julia, saying, "I am pleased to share in this great warmth," made a sketch in clay to memorialize their touching farewell.

The following morning, Silas made final preparations to return to Macedonia with a scroll of the newly re-written epistle of Peter. Before Peter would let them depart, he called Silas and Mauros into his quarters for a farewell kiss. He also had gifts: "Two for Silas and one for Mauros," he said. "Here is a pair of sandals for you, Mauros, and likewise a pair for my most helpful elder scribe. Also for you, Silas, this lovely seashell which I have kept with me since finding it off Caesarea in Samaria."

"Why a seashell, Cephas?" Silas asked.

"You will discover the answer some quiet hour in Macedonia, Silas. Place it to your ear from time to time."

They were soon packed and on their way back through Brundisium. At their first stopover, Silas confided to Mauros, "I shall not see Paul again, I suspect; nor Peter again, I fear, Mauros. Peter confided that he foresees his own death at the hand of the madman who rules the Empire, who let the city burn, and who has killed his own mother and his wife. Nero needs more love than I, Silas, can give."

"I had not previously thought love capable of fighting to take a victory over evil, Deacon," Mauros replied as they returned to their course on the way back to Berea.

Silas turned, suggesting, "Perhaps it is more fitting to think of love absorbing evil, but the process differs from the absorption of dyes and colorings by wool. Love's power is more positive than that; it marshals a gentle invasion of the soul, an active move, as I view it. It seems to exceed the passive ingestion of dark dyes by a white fabric.... Really, I am not an expert in fabrics nor in philosophy, so this is not an easy subject for me to discuss. However, Mauros, I am convinced of the excellence, the superiority, of love as a virtue, a power. I hope you will be willing to return to this discussion later."

Mauros said, "Oh, yes, quite willing. May I make one last comment, Deacon? It seems that evil changes when love touches it, right?"

Silas smiled to say, "Yes, Mauros, people who really love can reduce errors to ash. That provides a glowing inspiration for better tomorrows. Now, let us turn to our blankets for a good night's sleep before we take on tomorrow's duties back in Dyrrachium. Good night!" So, they slept after they had embarked from Brundisium.

They arrived at Dyrrachium after a stormy crossing of the Ionian Sea —wintry weather churning the waves and threatening them.

Titus, who lived near the pier, met them as they disembarked. Silas forgot whether or not they had prearranged that. "Did we agree that you would stay here throughout all the time we were away, so that you could —?"

"Oh, no, Silas, we didn't, and I couldn't, but we have a communication system that informs us, and I had daily prompting," Titus said. As they moved up from the landing, Matthias also joined them. These two took pride in reporting that they had found Heldaiah, the friend of Melana whom Silas tried to locate when he last passed through the port city. "Yes, Silas: Heldaiah. Well, actually, the woman found us upon learning that we were seeking her. I can't identify the person who told her; it seems not to matter. When she dropped by, she said that she will be available any evening at the big taverna near the grist mill."

"Good!" Silas said, "and I look forward to leaving Melana's gift with her." They had not reached their quarters when a woman stepped from the crowd and joined them. Titus and Matthias acknowledged her, but no man would have ignored her. She was a woman of striking beauty —one might say, almost overdone beauty.

With a show of some pride in having found the person Silas had

FEASTING WITH THE DEACON

sought, Titus brought her forward saying, "Look who materialized only yesterday! This is Heldaiah whom you are trying to locate, I believe. Meet Silas the Cook!" Silas moved to acquaint himself with his wife's friend.

"Of course: Heldaiah. Heldaiah! You are one of Melana's old friends from Alexandria, right?"

"Always thought I was, sir..... How's she anyway? And does she still do those naughty tricks?"

Though trusting, Silas slipped past the woman's question and looked away as he considered her connection to Melana. He answered, "Melana is in good health and happy, I can report. She and I are married, as you may know, and we live in Berea, near Thessalonica, with our children."

"She still the darlin' of Caleb and the sailors, too?"

A loyal husband, Silas again ignored her incorrect reference, remarking, "You, I understand from Melana, are in charge of the grist mill at the docks. Right?"

"Huh, yes, sir, I am the big babe at the mill, I guess you'd say," Heldaiah remarked. "Wanna see my place?"

"I would prefer to first visit your grist mill, Heldaiah", Silas told her. "May my friend Mauros and I visit your place of work?"

Heldaiah paused before replying, and then said something to the effect that it would not be fair to the other workers at the mill. "Ya know, not fair to interrupt them and expect them to keep to their allocated quota of output; ya unnerstan, don't ya?" She then volunteered, "After hours, after dark, I'd be glad to show ya aroun the mill, mebbe, if you could meet me at the taverna for a glass of wine and a platter."

Silas and Mauros moved along with her as she proceeded to the taverna, commenting, "I unnerstan that this place serves the best roast pork aroun the waterfront, but —oh my, I forgit, your kind don't eat pork..... Well, well, we shall see what else. What else, Silas sweetie?"

"Frankly, Heldaiah, I would eat anything that's well prepared, if you would join us. We do not hold so closely to the dietary laws, and I hope you won't emphasize such details. Let us look to your connection to Melana, most importantly, since Mauros and I will have to move on toward Edhessa and Berea by dawn."

"Sure, Sure, sweetie, but we need to fortify ourselves with some of the strong wines at the Ram and Lamb, and mebbe dance awhile and watch the weather, 'cause it's going to snow, real bad, tonight, and you'll want to rest your hansum bodies at my place."

"But, Heldaiah, we have adequate rooms," Silas reminded her. "We are staying overnight at Matthias's house. Mauros, if it is indeed going to snow heavily, I think we should simply move on there. Heldaiah, we will have to go on, and I will give Melana a good report about our finding you. All right?"

The Heldaiah-for-a-day said, "If ya go on to yer fren's house, that'll give me a free evening, but aren't ya goin to pay me for tonight's loss of income?"

On hearing Silas's negative reply to that suggestion, she stormed, "Well, at least give me the present Melana sent to me, for our old friendship's sake." "That item is with my effects which Matthias took to his home, Heldaiah," said Silas, "and I believe we'll just go on there, giving you back your evening to prepare to face the snow that you've predicted. So, farewell, and God bless you, woman."

She was not giving up. Snuggling up to Mauros, she invited him with an expectant, "Wouldn't you like to spend the night with the cousin of Cleopatra, sweetie?" But Mauros rebuffed her with a comment that surprised even Silas: "I do not favor intimacies with strangers, even a relative of the Egyptian queen, and despite the fact that I am traveling a lonely road."

She shrank back from Mauros's blunt comment, which first drew a smile from Silas, and then, hearing her wounded snarl, Deacon Silas sensed her injury and asked, "Do you not have a place to stay? Perhaps you would like for me to ask Titus, who often shelters visitors and passing travelers." The woman shrugged her shoulders and turned away.

They arranged a chilly parting. As they walked away, Silas commented to Mauros, "I know he has two travelers from Hibernia arriving tomorrow: Fiona the Fair and her brother, both outstanding cooks. That reminder gives me an idea."

In Berea, too, events were shaping a future, and one of those events was a messenger's arrival at Melana's door, urging her to come quickly to the household of Mauros, in Edhessa. "Was something amiss, some accident along the road Mauros and Silas had taken to Rome?" she asked, praying it away and arranging with Lydia and the neighbors to watch the house for the two days she would be away. When she returned to Berea, Caleb was on the prowl and greeted her with his habitual ways of aggression and insult. She smiled, said almost nothing to him, and ran back

FEASTING WITH THE DEACON

up the hillside to embrace her children, assuring them that nothing was wrong at Mauros's house, and that "all is well with your dear father, as far as I can determine." She went to bed dreaming that all with Silas was well indeed, although the deacon himself might not have realized it.

The evening of Melana's safe return to Berea was the last evening Silas planned to be in Dyrrachium. To set it in Dyrrachian memory and to repay his hospitality, Silas cooked a hearty meal of pigeon, vegetables and a peach compote —all carried in from Titus's store of provisions. It became a memorable occasion for all: Titus, Silas, Matthias, Mauros, and their intimates in that household. After finishing the meal, Silas took Titus aside and chatted briefly. Then they all went to bed, grateful to the Almighty for true friendships blanketed in proper love.

However, sometime after midnight, a vision or dream woke Silas and he began to ponder on the woman at the waterfront. Heldaiah.... By the time the first rosiness of dawn bathed the edges of the southbound clouds, Silas was seen scouting around the dock area, near the collection of tavernas, looking for 'Heldaiah.' Someone saw him and apparently recognized him as her accomplice from the preceding day, since she shortly materialized beside him in the harbor mist. "Well, dear deacon! Ya had second thoughts about a dance between mah legs, right?" she teased.

"No, Heldaiah, not about that temptation, but second thoughts about you. I do not want to go back to Melana without reaching a better conclusion than we had seen yesterday."

"Ye-e-ehsss?? And wot would ya wanna reach?" she asked.

"A truth.... I do not believe you are Heldaiah. What is your true name? Who set you on this task, this assignment to seduce Mauros and me?"

"I'm not free to talk about it; he paid me to keep silent on his friendship with yer Melana," she said, "an' —oh, wat's th use? I really am Tamara, daughter of a runaway Egyptian woman and her sailor from Alexandria. Ah growed up wi' that crowd."

"Come with me, Tamara, to the house of Titus. Titus agreed to provide lodging for you for a time."

"Fer a time? An' then wot? An wot else?" she asked with no little suspicion reflected.

Silas said, "Titus will offer you shelter and warm lodging, loving companions, and a chance to learn a new occupation. I call it 'holy intervention.'"

As they walked, Tamara seemed willing to at least consider the proposition. She asked, "Will there be other women there?"

Silas's reply was that a traveling cook from Hibernia, one Fiona Fair, was expected the next day. "I hope that friendship and shared interests will attract you to work with her."

"Cook, eh? Work with Fi-o-na, eh?." She turned it over in her mind. "Might not be such a bad idea'; and they stopped at Titus's doorway, where Silas's knock brought the owner. Titus and Tamara exchanged introductions and coolly discussed arrangements before Silas took final farewells. Then he went on to Matthias's house to finish the night and patch some more sleep into it. Too soon for Silas came the chilly dawn. He and Mauros saw that the north wind had slackened, not making snow. Following loving farewells and shared words of blessing with the household of Matthias, the Bereans headed out of Dyrrachium. They and their donkey moved along the paths that led to the eastbound Egnatian Road, pointing onward, to home and family for both of them.

Silas was quiet for the first hour or so on the road, contemplating the ways love reaches out to straying sinners, embracing them. 'With continuing concern and loving affection," he concluded, "the strays themselves become the essence of love. Errors fall away to virtues when glowing robes of love capture them, taking them inside.' So he told himself....

Finally he spoke. "Erring changes us, opens us.... These occasions are like nothing else, do you not agree?" the deacon asked, his eyes a-twinkle, his smile alight. Mauros made some noises of consent but seemed to have formed new questions of his own, which led to discussions all the way back through Edhessa and on to Berea. For example, he asked about the nature of special prophets and figures such as Christ. "To be specific, Deacon, how did he differ from such heroes as the great Alexander, our homegrown deity?"

Silas took time to consider this important question, beginning his response with an escape to exceptions: "Well, Alexander was human, and that is the chief difference, I believe. However, you make a good point: Alexander did preserve all that he and his officers found workable. He made positive moves in the blending of peoples —forcing his Greek and Macedonian officers to marry Asian women. He created formulas for peace, helped the conquered people to find new lives as freedmen, and fostered a good society where the best principles were united. We may have lost a great statesman by his premature death, but that is a common claim. However, I am convinced he was not a god, which is where Jesus easily fits. Watch and pray."

Next morning, Silas formulated a long speech of regrets to Melana. On the remaining travel to Berea, he made Mauros uneasy by his long face and his repentances at every possible stop. With meditation and hard work along the way, however, he had recovered quite well by the time they arrived at the home of Mauros in Edhessa. Mauros's wife seemed almost as happy seeing Silas as she was in greeting the returning Mauros, and all were prayerfully glad. In their rejoicing, they formed loving farewells the following morning, sending Silas charging toward the northeast slopes of Mount Vermion —the elevation that provided a lodging place for the village of Berea.

Even as he arrived back in Berea, Silas met Caleb, who confronted him: "Well, Deacon Devout, I heard that you sought out the beautiful Heldaiah...!"

Silas acknowledged, "Yes, I did go looking for her, since she is a long-time friend of Melana's, as you would know."

"Oh yes, Silas, I know that Heldaiah, and very well I do!" He smirked, adding, "I know her well enough to assert that your visit with her ended in her bed, and not alone. So much for your chaste behavior! Your recruits will be noising this scandal as soon as we it get organized."

"You have no scandal, Caleb. There is no truth in what you claim, friend. I am sure that Melana, as well as your false Heldaiah will testify to my statement, which I am pleased to say has several witnesses. Have you so little to occupy your time that you waste your days on earth constructing a fabric of lies such as this?"

Caleb murmured some comment such as "Just you wait and see, and wait and see Melana's face when she finds out! Oh, here she comes now."

Silas was delighted to see his dear wife and joined Caleb in welcoming her. "Yes, let us clear the matter up with her, since it is her love that I wish to preserve: that and the love of God. Melana, please tell us what you can of your friend Heldaiah, whom I failed to find in Dyrrachium. Caleb is trying to blackmail me on Heldaiah's behalf, because he thinks he has grounds to do so," Silas reported.

"Naw, no-no, not blackmail, Deacon," Caleb groused, facing Melana with his hand on his crotch as usual.

As she joined them, Melana smiled at both men and then turned to Caleb. "Caleb, never again approach me or my daughters with your obscenity flag waving across your loins like that. Do you hear? Never! If prayer has not prevented your insults, perhaps my strong kick, well placed, will teach you —" She aimed a foot above his thigh, as he cringed away, and Silas, smiling, restrained her lovingly.

Then Melana sternly inquired, "Now, what would you two wish to know about Heldaiah? She, my long-time friend, is on her way by boat to Alexandria, even as we speak."

Both men seemed speechless as they tried to absorb that news, which Melana explained, waving them to sit and sternly pressing her finger to her lip. "Be still and listen, both of you. I received a message telling me to meet Heldaiah in Edhessa, and I went, knowing nothing of the mess you conspired to cook, Caleb, even as I still do not know. Here are the most recent facts for both of you to consider: Heldaiah came through to Edhessa from Dyrrachium and was on her way to Alexandrian by way of Thessalonica and Athens. She is simply going to join her husband, who is harpist for the proconsul in Alexandria. It is the same post he held in Dyrrachium, earlier."

Melana sat down beside Silas and addressed Caleb the Obscene, suggesting, "I would like to have some privacy with Silas now, Caleb. Please leave us alone." When they were alone, Melana told Silas about a bundle of surprises, including that her friend Heldaiah had passed through, finding Melana almost by accident. As it turned out, Heldaiah was simply hiking back to Athens and destined to Alexandria, again. She was rejoining her harpist husband. She had said, and —according to Melana, Heldaiah added, "We sing together, but as Silas foresaw, I have formulated a hybrid Jewish/Buddhist religion, ultimately pointing to the one true God, but by what human author, I do not know." Thereupon, Silas allowed that rivers also hybridize, and all may lose their names as they become the ocean: one ocean and one God.

Melana and Silas envisioned some of the tests lay ahead. All their insight into the nature of God and mankind would be severely tested and demonstrated in the immediate future; it did not require a certified seer to recognize that prospect.

CHAPTER 10.

(A.D.68) —PETER AND PAUL AND NERO

(Silas, 60; Melana, 44; Lydia, 12; Joshua, 11; Johara, 4)

"Pray for those who render harm; otherwise, how will Love win Satan? as Love shall in the end!"—Epistle of Silas/

A SADNESS AT BEREA

'Bring scandal or rewards,' ran an old Nabatean saying, 'and we shall honor you with a moment's consideration!'. Scandal moved out of Rome on that morning as the saddening news reached Berea; rewards required a wait. Scandal arrived, sandal-footed, enormous and imperial —by messenger. More than a moment's consideration would be given.

A man and a woman, Thessalonians in sandals, had appeared at the door and spoken to Melana; they were soon gone, too quickly to permit hospitality. As they turned back down the path, Lydia, who had been watching them, noticed that they wore small wooden crosses on their garments.

Had they come to announce plans for a festivity at the mission? Not likely, she decided; they were too quiet, their faces, too somber —almost sorrowing. Before she could construct possibilities for their behavior, she heard her mother's call: 'Lydia, Joshua!' and took her brother's hand as they went to the house. Johara, now four years old, was content to stay outside; she and a neighbor's son continued playing with Melana's new cat, Skepsi.

Skepsi had been a mere kitten when Melana first saw it in the pouring rain last year, when it reminded her of the Sheban cat that had given her such pleasure as a girl in Alexandria. Dismissing that thought with a sad smile, she asked her older children, "Please sit down; we have just received shockingly sad news." Then she told Joshua and Lydia about Nero's visit to Corinth, and disclosed the deaths of Paul and their father's friend, Peter.

Few of the community in Berea had met Paul; still fewer, Peter. Fewer yet had assimilated Paul; fewest of all were those who had first-hand knowledge of the Emperor. Nero was said to have decided to rename the southern districts Neronesos, replacing the Peloponesos. Not many Bereans would recognize the fact that the Roman emperor was a terrorist who had now invaded the minds as well as the territory of his subjects. Now he was to visit the provinces, according to the report from Thessalonica. So what? Yet, how much do you children and I ever attend to the deeds, injuries or joys of anyone beyond the confines of Berea?

"We ought to have a memorial for them," Melana proposed, "a little prayer ceremony and meal of crisp breads and honest vegetables, crisp and honest, such as those men were. If you will gather the peas and greens, I will make dark breads. Your father will soon return from his visitation to the community at Edhessa."

Joshua volunteered, "I will first start the fire in the backyard baking oven, Mother. I can do that. ('You may become a builder, Dosh,' Silas had forecast last year, 'like Joseph of Nazareth.') He could build a thrifty fire, too, and bring it to oven heat fast. It was only a short time, then, before he joined his sisters in the garden. Lydia was very quiet; Johara sobbed. She could not understand it all, but Johara knew Lydia's face, and it showed an almost unbearable loss.

"Paulos is ended," she told Joshua when he rejoined them.

"Yes, Johara. Petros, too."

Three children huddled there —circled in a hugging prayer —in a garden on that sunny Berean hillside, reaching for the love of God.

Decorating that garden, a pair of maroon-feathered *Kolibrion* hummingbirds courted the most dazzlingly configured and painted flowers. A delight to the eyes and a wonder to the ear, the hummingbirds were, as the watching children pondered a distant grief.

After a pause, drying eyes, they were back to the task of collecting crisp greens and snap peas. Thus were the children in the garden when Silas came up the lane, merrily chanting:

`O Nero rules the stage of fools,
Miscast, he rules at Rome!`

FEASTING WITH THE DEACON

His Empire is his stage.`
But here in Greece, we keep the peace;
In truth, Here, Peace is home;
`Here peace and love engage.'

"Papa! You're home before we have the special meal ready!" Lydia exclaimed, interrupting his silly song.

"Special meal?" Silas queried. "Do you and your dear mother plan a special meal in honor of the Emperor?"

"No, no. Just a quiet special meal to honor Paul and our dearest Cephas," Lydia replied.

"Oh, I see," replied Silas, not comprehending the intended news. Apparently fascinated by the hummingbirds, he commented, "What lovely *Kolibri* you have attracted. Marvels of flight, they can fly backwards —fast, too, as all of you probably know ...."

He then slipped into the cottage. Obviously, if he was a bit confused, Melana would help him segregate and examine the news reaching Berea. She was arranging a simple display of flowers, dried spices and white ribbons on the bare dark wood of the table.

His wife looked up at Silas from her preparations of small breads and fresh vegetables. They hugged: Silas, Melana, Melana, Silas, arms welcoming again. Suddenly, he turned and burst out, "Melana, everyone in Edhessa sends greetings! Here are some late turnips from Mauros and his wife. The little church is built, rather drafty it will be in a winter chill; windy and cold up there by the falls. Everyone remembers you and the children."

Not stopping, Silas sped his tongue: "That is part of the news. But have you heard about Nero? He's to be in Corinth soon!" Melana and Joshua gave Silas looks that seemed to urge him on, but also reflected concerned astonishment. Did he not understand the message from Rome? The family rode through the sort of communication failure that is beyond remedy until a pause steps in, to cut through the noise.

Lydia tried: "Papa! Papa!!' But she cut short her interruption. She concluded that an interruption to bring news about the mad Emperor might simply enlarge their dread of the ruler's madness. Taking a cue from Melana's silence she let Silas continue.

"Nero has sent a part of his entourage to Athens", the deacon reported. "They are to meet his ship when it docks at Piraeus in less than a week. Then —are we ready for this? He is to grant Corinth its freedom again. He has ordered an enormous festival. I think that would be a marvelous time for several of this family to go to Corinth. Wouldn't you like to go, Melanasha? In Edhessa, many speak of it. Caravan after caravan has been passing through on the Egnatian Way. They say crowds are also en route to Corinth from Thessalonica. What do you say?" Finally, Silas removed his dusty petasos, struck it against the door sill, and waited for his wife to speak.

"Husband, you have not heard the other news from Rome?" Melana took advantage of the pause all of them had awaited; now it was her turn to complete the report. "Silas, both Paul and Peter were put to death by Nero's officers last year. They are dead and buried in Rome, my love. Runners from the church at Thessalonica have just left our door, after telling me the terrible news."

Now, the entire household felt it; the love that had knit the new faith had been strained by apostasies and torn by neighbors' deaths before, but not put at such risk as the loss of Peter and Paul invoked. Silas turned away and briefly wept.

"Oh, bless their souls; they both served well," Silas declared, wiping his eyes of tears. He, for a moment, was overcome, as were Lydia, Joshua and Melana. Johara asked if souls are dead and buried, and Lydia assured her little sister that "Peter's soul and Paul's soul have by now taken up singing in Paradise, praising God. Right, Mama?"

Melana agreed with Lydia, noting that the two servants had helped mold and shape a new spiritual community. Now others would forge paths for the flight of souls; new recruits would have to learn to guide fledgling believers to the glorification of God. "Otherwise" Melana foresaw, "future children might miss glorifying opportunities, and —failing —also miss the opportunity to be picked up in mystery and be blessed for their child-like ways."

Silas and Melana joined their children then, for a short memorial, a meal marked by its crisp and honest vegetables and the awareness of Paul and Cephas as rarities. But, as Joshua remarked, "Surely, Nero is a rarity, too."

"Yes," Silas strongly agreed, "and so ready to be conquered and healed by love."

FEASTING WITH THE DEACON

"I am not open to that suggestion, or perhaps I am not yet wealthy enough in the spirit to agree to it," Melana demurred.

That evening, the deacon's family shared the sad news with other Bereans and helped them accommodate to its weight. Lydia helped arrange a prayer service and knelt with friends before commemorative candles. The mood slowly moderated and turned to joy; joy found songs to displace the thick silence of mourning that darkened other houses at other times. "More fitting," Silas said.

Two days after the collected news from Rome was assimilated, Melana and Silas had decided to hurry on to Corinth to try to arrange a meeting with Nero. They had elected to take Lydia, which Joshua and Johara understood and accepted quite well. Caleb and Zayda had agreed to take care of them while Lydia and her parents made the two-week round trip.

Lydia was overjoyed: "I shall see the Emperor's carnival and maybe the Emperor himself."

"Bring us some relic of your visit there," her brother commanded. "Yes, oh yes!" cheered Johara, "Perhaps a lovely scarf or a comb. Just don't forget us."

However, on the second morning of the trip, when they prepared to embark by boat from the landing near the Pydna ruins, Silas and Melana had deliberated further. In the course of their careful consideration, they concluded that Lydia should not go on to Corinth, but return to Berea. "We want you to take charge of the house and the younger ones, Lydia. I admit, we are disappointed that you will not be with us in this rare encounter, but we are also quite concerned about rumors that Nero's troops graze on lovely young women. Your father doubts we could protect you among the mob at Corinth," Melana told her. "If we cannot do so, we must take this precaution at some annoyance for all of us."

"Mother, this is a terrible way to treat me!" Lydia protested. "Like a baby who has to be wrapped in blankets —yet still your daughter who acts as a big sister for your little ones, playing nursemaid to Joshua and Johara."

Lydia let her anger grow: "What am I, a toy for you? If Nero sends his men for my body, we can depend on a miracle to save me, can't we? You claim we can pray for whatever we need; are you now showing your doubts? What am I to believe?"

"You can believe our devotion to God and our desire for your happiness, Lydia," Silas said firmly. "Now, show your concern for your own safety and our happiness, and say a prayer of thanks that you exist and can worship correctly. We return you in good company to a safe home where we shall rejoin you a week after the festival ends. You can rely on it, you will have a set of souvenirs, if only legends. You may sell some of the eggplants from the garden; I know they will be just right for the merchant brokers coming through Berea from Thessalonica."

Happily, Lydia's fury cooled quickly. She smiled into her father's eyes; she touched the crown of his rumpled petasos —"Funny hat, Papa!"— then she took Melana's hand. Both parents hugged their disgruntled daughter and sent her on her way back along the short distance through the wild country northerly from Olympos to the solid safety of Berea.

Then they walked toward the boatman: Lysimachus was again their captain! After greetings, they found places for their baggage and for themselves on the tiny vessel, southbound to a landing at Cenchrae.

Four days later, they fully disembarked at the east end of the gulch leading to Corinth; even there, five miles from the festival city, Nero's troops patrolled the area. Seeing the heavy investment in guards, Silas suggested that they should arrange for an official convoy to the presence of the emperor. Melana said, "I think our safety would be well assured if we could get the officer you told me about: Tobias Publius—the man who came with you from Corinth to Berea."

That seemed a very logical suggestion, so they proceeded to tackle those arrangements as soon as possible. Accordingly, Silas asked to speak to the most senior officer who shortly appeared, requiring Silas to affirm his claim to Roman citizenship. "Not bought, my good captain, but born to it," Silas cheered himself. Then he and Melana urged on the officer their serious petition to meet with the Emperor for discussions of 'matters of overriding importance,' as they expressed it.

"I make no promises but will convey your request," the officer remarked, conforming to the sense and syntax of a consummate Roman bureaucrat. "I see by your papers that you are the son of my old commander in Jerusalem, Titus Gaddiel Lucanius. What a genius he was! Is he still living, I hope?"

"No, he died some —oh, almost 20 years past, thank you."

"Well, benGaddiel, I have most excellent memories of your father, and yes, I shall convey your request for the an audience with the Emperor, although that is such a rare arrangement —"

FEASTING WITH THE DEACON

"Excellent!" Silas replied, "We understand that we are asking a truly special privilege, but we are going to expand that request: We also ask that you announce our presence here to our friend, the Cornicular Zaccur Tobias Publius."

"Oh, we know him, and he is here," said the officer. "I shall do all that I can to bring you to your connections."

"God bless you," said Melana. "Now, do we have your name, so that we may learn the outcome of this request?"

"Ask for Cato, my code name," the captain said.

"Very well," Silas acknowledged, lifting the brim of his petasos enough to reinforce recognition when it would be required. "We shall look for you at the main entrance of the theater." Silas and Melana then picked up their belongings, found a young man to hire as a bearer of them, and set out for the edge of Corinth. It turned into a hard walk of about an hour.

TERROR AT CORINTH

Corinth teemed. Arrival at the city during a festival sharpened Silas's memories of its characteristics, not all of them unpleasant. Compared with Corinth, Berea —even at fairs and other celebrations —provided a loving neighborhood, an enclave for contemplation. "We need both," Melana reminded him when he commented on the difference. Instead of reminiscing, however, he and Melana must find the house of Prisca and Aquila, a house which had become the major haven for believers in the Way when they found themselves transients in Corinth. One did not have to make arrangements there because visitors were always expected.

Today is another such time, and Prisca hurries to embrace Silas and Melana to welcome them: "Seems only last week that I attended your beautiful wedding in Berea, but what is the purpose of your presence in Corinth at this unusual time?"

Melana smiles, saying, "We will want to hear more comments on the calendar and on time." She adds, "Is any time a usual time in Corinth?"

"Well, more about that matter later, but you do carry courage and the love of God to admirable extremes," Aquila observes, adding in warning, "My friends at the consul's office tell me Nero has worked out a routine, a little dramatic skit aimed to insult those of us who have adopted the Way. They say he composed the script after his last conversations with Paul, just before he chopped our friend's bald head away. I would not seek an audience with him, as you two have done."

"Why? How can we ever capture evil-doers if we do not challenge them? Embrace them? Surround their circle of hate with a larger circle, framed of love?" Silas asks firmly.

Priscilla speaks. "Corinthians have seen more of his terror than you have, and I truly fear Nero is beyond hope, irredeemable."

Making a point, Silas counters with an assertion that "the Emperor is irredeemable only if he denies his possible redemption," to which Aquila and Prisca both nod in seeming sadness.

Melana declares, "We intend to praise God by urging the Emperor to seek insight to grace, but we are frail, too; Silas and I realize that we may not succeed in this case. Perhaps, though, we can make plantings.... Shall we go to the big event? I see it is nearly dusk."

The intersection of the path with the Lechaion Road was crowded, reflecting the widespread interest in Nero's performance. Groups of patrolling soldiers on the Lechaion also showed the Roman army's conclusion that the Emperor required substantial protection. So many people were en route to the Corinthian theater that Prisca pulled back and asked Aquila to return with her to their home. "This crush and rabble will be more than I can take!" she declared. "You and Silas go on, if you insist. We will wait prayerfully for your return; perhaps we will have the opportunity of hearing about the Emperor's reply to your preachings."

Melana turned to take Prisca's hands in hers. "Your dread is probably well founded. Thank you for the comfort of your prayers and good wishes; be assured, we will hurry right back to your door when the spectacle ends."

Crowds densified with their every step nearer the theater. Altogether, the gathering had become a packed throng as Silas and Melana approached the entrances to the theater. Dust swirled in clouds around the colorful flags the edile had provided to welcome the emperor. Melana overheard a soldier say that Nero had already jailed the edile for failing to add rose blossoms to the baths. "Probably execute him if anything else goes contrary this evening," the soldier added before Melana moved out of earshot.

Now, they were at the main entrance, and aware that everyone received directions and controls before they could take seats. The movement slowed further; Silas looked around. Who could they approach in their search for the officer called Cato? Cato materialized from the group of military officials at the gate and came forward. "We have made some progress," he

FEASTING WITH THE DEACON

said, "I am happy to report. You may sit in the second row, center, at the aisle! No better view in the theater."

"You know that we thank you for this accommodation," Melana stated. "Yes," Silas added, continuing her assertion, "how did you arrange it?"

"I suppose I should claim personal influence," Cato announced, "but the Emperor actually asked us to include you in this way. I identified you to him. Your boat captain at the Cenchraean landing told me you are a temple ruler. So, you are known to Nero himself as 'the Berean-Temple Wayfarers-in-the-second-row.' Now come. I shall seat you myself."

Silas and Melana observed that they were being marked, and the marking was surely not intended to honor them. "Well, while we pray and wait, let us be thankful that we did not have to fight off the promoters for a seat," Silas suggested. Melana smiled and took his hand.

Just as Melana and Silas finished adjusting to their seats on the bench, four musicians appeared onstage; their trumpeting announced the arrival of Nero.

The Emperor swiftly took control of the stage. He did not say he was pleased to be there. He quite simply proclaimed that Corinth was once again a free city; "Now, behave yourselves, or I shall have to drown your pets and burn your houses." And he giggled, then lifted his hands outstretched, inviting the crowd to laugh with him. "Laugh, Corinthians! It is my policy; I require it. Romans now find my edicts and orders quite amusing."

Some laughter followed.

Nero interrupted the light laughter. "Obviously, you do not enjoy my little humor; perhaps you will enjoy my larger humor. Now, stay right there; I shall return in less than three minutes with the most divine performance you ever saw. I designed it for all of the misled Jews and so-called Christians who are with us this evening. While I am preparing, the candle lighters will bring more lamps and candles around the stage here; thus you may see the superb and most extravagant act I shall perform for you.

"Oh, before I go, do my servants inform me correctly that Silas and his black bride are in the second row, and the chief rabbi of this newly freed city is behind them in the fourth row? Will all three of you please stand, so I can be sure?"

Was this it? Was this the ridicule Nero reputedly dumped on those least in favor in court, surely including Jews and those who had chosen the Way? Well, all three of them answered Nero's request; better to acknowledge who they were than to deny their identity, and lose it. They stood.

"Now," Nero crowed, "there they are. I must say, I wonder how serious Silas's bride is about her new religion, since she once practiced our divinities when she lived in Alexandria. Oh, how fickle are the Nubian women! Even so, we must get the theater of the evening underway.... As a starter exercise to practice, I want all the rest of you to boo. Say 'boo.'" The audience obeyed with a spoken 'boo.' Nero shouted, "Not that whisper! Louder! Let me hear 'Boo'! rather loud."

Again, the audience obeyed, but louder the second time.

Nero giggled and doubled over with laughter, applauding the effort. "That is sufficient for the moment. I shall be back in a twinkling," Nero promised. "Now, stay right there. Heh, heh." And he slipped to the edge of the stage, out of view.

During Nero's brief absence, uneasiness spread among the group nearest Silas and Melana. The woman next murmured, "I, too, am a follower of the Way."

The man behind Melana tapped Silas on the shoulder: "And I am a Jew; what is to be done?"

"Pray!" Silas replied, as a trumpeting began again....

Three figures began moving from the darker edge of the stage, and two of them separated from the figure in the center. Bursting into view they took further shape as a naked man and a naked woman, turning cartwheels to-and-fro across the stage, accompanied by a drum beat. The drumming increased in cadence and intensity, ultimately dissolving into indistinguishability. By then, the acrobats had disappeared and, in the strongest glow of the lamplight, the third figure, a crudely garbed Nero, danced, his face painted with a mixture of garish colors.

Nero's dance gave a suggestion of sensuality, and his figure made a pretense to pregnancy. With stuffing under his robes and belly protruding, the Emperor struck a pose of mock maternity. "I am Claudia Drusus, eternal virgin, elect of the gods to bear a god for you all to worship. See! my time of labor approaches with the birth of a new god for the Jews. Oh, I hope its birth brings pleasure to my rabbi and our so-called Christians. I am quite certain that that pleasure will not equal that which its conception brought me." He lowered his eyes and covered his mouth in a pretense of shyness, feigning shock at his own remark.

FEASTING WITH THE DEACON

Nero reminded the audience, "Now, this is a time to be very quiet. A god is about to be delivered from the furnaces of my marvelous body.... I shall spread my legs quite properly and serve as my own assistant, and, and —now you must watch carefully —there, beautiful, ahh, a truly beautiful god for you."

In that turn and squirm of his clothing, Nero extracted from the wrappings a squealing, newborn pig which he pinched and squeezed. He held it up for admiration. Again, he opened his free arm for applause and cheers, cupping his ear to show that he expected —required! —a greater response. A mixture of cheers and silences dotted the crowd. Melana prepared to stand. Two muscular bodyguards materialized, one on either side of the Emperor.

Seeing her movement so close to the stage, one guard began to step toward the threat Melana appeared to pose —her anger showing. Nero seemed to anticipate this sequence of responses, and, without looking directly at her, said, "You Wayfaring believers may regard this trick a pale reflection of a divinity's ability. Let me assure you, however, you are correct. We can do better.

"Stay right where you are. This is a top act, a gilded prize-winner. All you false believers deserve to see the best." (This last comment was thrown at Melana, who continued to watch in anger.)

Nero, with nimble assistance from bodyguards, tied the pig with a rope binding. With exaggerated tenderness and ugly cooings, he placed the squealing animal into a makeshift cradle. After a few seconds, the confused piglet stopped squealing. Nero bowed deeply to the crowd. He turned, ever so slowly then, turned and lifted his robe. He bowed again, deeply, but away from the audience, baring his backside.

When the roar of the crowd subsided, Nero faced them with a question: "Does anyone have a knife the Emperor might borrow? Ahh, here is a knife," he acknowledged, "A right sharp one, thank you. Watch; we are going to convert this baby god into a genuine spirit, the truest of Messiahs, as you call them, I believe. First, we must make the little boy pig into a good Jew. My duty, now, is to perform its circumcision. Let me find its tiny poker, and —there, all done! —we have a first-class Jew. I think," he added, giggling, "I think it is a Pharisee, so strictly does it obey my law."

He held the pig into the brighter light. "Ah, isn't he divine? What a fulgent god he makes! But a radiance still greater will come, dear friends.

"While I, your little Roman virgin, travailed and brought forth this marvelous little god," Nero declared, "some kind helpers put this structure together." He lifted a wooden cross into view and arranged it on a platform stand quite near him.

"Corinthians, I need your cooperation. I have brought this little being to a condition approaching perfect godhood, but we need to take a few more steps. To accomplish this, you must shout: 'Crucify him.' Let me hear you say it. Oh, not so good. You are poor shouters. Louder; louder yet: 'Crucify him.' And again, 'Crucify him!' I said."

The Corinthian crowd left their fearfulness behind; the infection of a festival took root and spread among the crowd. Many shouted, "Crucify, crucify him!" Melana and Silas bowed and prayed, pressing their heads gently close, to give each other assurance of two gathered-together.

As the shouting call continued, Nero took the piglet from its cradle bindings. With a flourish he began to rope its forefeet to the upper arms of the little wooden cross; that finished, he tied its rear legs together and then bound them to the lower shaft. Then he stood back from his work, shouting, "Behold your god!"

Nero rushed at the pig with the borrowed knife and slashed the animal's throat, taking its blood into his robe. The struggling piglet began its death throes and then died, whimpered squeak. An uneasiness began and propagated itself throughout the audience.

Melana sensed a movement by Silas. Her eyes followed him as he rose. "Stop! End this terrible mockery!" Silas shouted, standing. Guards rushed at him, since his seat was at the aisle.

"No, let the man alone," Nero commanded. "That fellow is Silas, who has a devotion to the god of his friend Paul. Poor fellow, Paul. Like Silas, standing now here before you, Paul was a Roman citizen, crying 'Caesare appello!' every time, when he was in trouble. But Paul made the mistake of disputing my godhood, putting the Jewish Jesus forward falsely, as God. Silas, we had been expecting to hear from you, since you were known as a *higoumen*, a leader long ago in the Jordan Valley, right? Before I go on, do you have anything more to say?"

"Emperor, I ask that you cease this obscenity —that we all repair to the true God, and mend our ways."

"Overruled, *Higoumen!*" Nero announced. "We have much more enjoyable tasks ahead. If you are truly a leader, a *higoumen*, ask the audience if they would not wish more of this drama. Audience! You want more, do you not? Say 'more'!"

"More, more!" came some half-hearted cries.

"More is what you shall have, despite this silly deacon's protest. You certainly deserve anything the Emperor offers, especially to any of your young maidens who may wish to see me privately later.... Now, for my closing, I must have your undivided attention. You will all find this edifying, I am sure."

He turned the wooden cross to face the audience, the piglet now limply attached. "You see this god, now dead," he said. "You must want him alive again. He shall return. Verily, he shall fly to a new form! It is my privilege to assure that you witness him rise from the dead."

He untied the light ropes that held the pig to the cross and embraced the gory animal. "Now, you beautiful worker of wonders, rise. Rise from the dead!"

He held the pig away from the cross, its bloody head drooping across its chest. He held it for the audience to study.

"I direct you, rise, little god; give these people something to really remember. Rise, Rise!" So shouting, Nero leaned back to gain enough thrust to elevate the pig's body, propelling it toward the audience. The piglet rose away from the stage in a short arc and bounced off the back of a man in the third row, falling into the rabbi's lap. The rabbi stood, took off his garments, and vomited on the pig.

Nero giggled again.

Melana stood and moved rapidly in Nero's direction. "You, you must stop this! What terrible acts these are —you have given us a complete catalog of evil and wickedness. But, my Emperor, there is a better path, a higher road. Your conversion to the Way of the Master would construct spiritual banquets across the Empire. Pray and believe. Pray, as we pray for you. Else, I foresee —as does my husband, Silas the Prophet and *Higoumen* —I foresee that you shall soon develop a fatal disgust for the state of your soul. If you want to have a joyful life instead of death from some evil hand, perhaps your own, simply accept the gift of grace. It would be so easy!"

"Remove her!" Nero demanded, pushing at two of his guards. Silas rushed to join his wife in a defensive move. With her left hand, Melana took Silas firmly by the right elbow. Nero's guards approached rapidly, menacingly. Facing them just ahead of Silas, Melana saw her chance to escape prospective capture. Pulling on Silas, she turned her right shoulder into the chin of the slightly-built soldier at her right, then released Silas' hand. In a similar lightning twist, Silas caught a second guard off balance and sent him reeling into the crowd that had drawn in around the confrontation.

Melana had sparked a riot!

Although Roman guards rushed to quench it, they were confused by blocked aisles and their compulsion to draw a circle around the Emperor, to protect him. Nero, however, roared with laughter, hardly requiring or expecting protection. The guard commander, hearing the laughter, grew further confused. "Where did the offenders go? What did they look like?"

As Silas considered their escape, he saw a familiar face among the officer guards who seemed to connive in frustrating the guards. Could it be, was it perhaps, Zaccur Tobias? If it was not the Cornicular, the fact that he tripped two other guards during the next seconds made it a rather comic chase.

To anticipate the chase, Silas had removed his petasos; in a flash, he handed it to Melana. Melana turned away from the main body of guards, stopped and placed the hat at a sharp angle on her own head. Then she lowered her glance and raised herself into a queenly position. In such a regal pose, she moved at a nobly slow pace with the crowd. Silas hurried, bareheaded, beyond her. At the entrance to the theater, he found an usher's niche. Awaiting Melana, he stood enclosed in semi-darkness, praying silent utterances of praise.

When Melana came abreast of the entranceway, Silas slipped beside her, muttering, "Lovely petasos, woman child!"

"You will notice that it carries a burden of sweat, man child!" she cautioned, placing the hat back on Silas' head. Then they briefly held one another, hugging to the point of bringing a sharp pain to their shoulders.

Borrowing a glance from love, Melana and Silas then joined hands and ran down from the theater. A cue for directions came in sight as they hastened, and Silas recognized that his old friend (this time, there was no doubt!) Zaccur Tobias was standing to retard any chase that might be organized against them. Tobi smiled broadly as they ran on. They ran, panting, past the agora to the secret cave Silas knew beneath the house where Aquila and Prisca lived.

FEASTING WITH THE DEACON

Two days later, Nero dedicated the area as the *Neronesus:* 'Nero's Islands,' displacing the revered old name of Peloponesus and drawing anger from some Greek partisans. Others, scraping favor, arranged to add laurels to the head of the tyrant by insulting God and honoring Nero with the title *Zeus Eleutherios,* or Liberating God. Altogether, the result was a rumor of the Greek people's prospective revolt. Moving to counter the outcome, Nero assigned his guards back near the ship that would take him back to Rome. By that time, friends such as Lysimachus could assure Silas, "Nero has moved on with his carnival. Corinth is now again a safe haven for you and Melana."

Melana and Silas packed for the return to Berea. From several sources, Prisca and Aquila had already heard about those events at the theater stage; such wildness creates the kinds of performance Corinthians remember!

Wanting to bring back souvenirs from Corinth to Lydia and the younger children, as she had implied she would, Melana asked Priscilla for a suggestion. "I shall do better than suggest. There is nothing like Aquila's spicy currant cookies to keep reminding you of Corinth. Here is a basketful with our love." As they started off toward the hidden boat-landing with their memories of Corinth and their cookies for the children, Prisca told Silas that he had a whole bagful of fortune, topped by Melana. Silas knew that, all along.

CHAPTER II.

MYSTERIES OF WATER

(Lydia is 13; Joshua, 12; Johara, 6.)

\"Love and other forces of the Spirit do not exist alone, in solitude; they gather sinews and strength as the number sharing them."—Epistle of Silas/

※※※

Silas slept; he slept a hybrid sleep of memories and mysteries, some converting to dreams; undreamt and clouded dreams pulled time's blanket down a damp slope of space, visions sketched on his mind by God's moistened fingernail. He moved toward wakefulness. Dreams now poured out, dreams of pressing vapors and gushing water, noises breaking the silence. In his dreaming, Silas inserted himself into the utter silences of God's first instant, before the waters formed. He now saw the Act that gathered God's energies into small and perfect fragments.

Silas beheld those particulate fragments forming and creating time, earth and the tidal oceans. In half-sleep, Silas witnessed that Act. Wanting to see more, he pulled at the edges of space to get a better view, but the view dissolved into the cascades that fell away from the height, fell away in every direction. Then the dream broke on the anvil of thunder and rushing waters....

'Yes, yes, it was a rushing sound,' Silas assured himself as he came awake to a rushing roar.

Wakening to a torrential rain, he detached himself fully from his dream and felt overcome by an ancient thirst; he tried to master a dry sense of separation. Was he alone on a desert island enclosed by stormy seas? He lifted himself into the Berean reality, concluding that he was not alone. He said his 'glorias.' Then Silas stood, made his way slowly across the straw-covered floor, and peered out the door at the weather.

Water, rushing, pushed out of the passing clouds; somewhat overdue, it gushed as from a porous vessel, overhead and skyborne, but most speedily. Floods sent by night from a lightning-wounded cloud bank attacked Berea in the light of dawn's brightening flares. Thunder thumped, tearing more rain from new wounds in that ragged range of clouds; there was not enough time between strokes of lightning for the cloud bank to mend and seal its leaking seams. Trees toppled in a heavy wind descending Mt. Vermion's slopes. Streets became streams.

Slowly, the thunder drums grew distant; slowly, they moved easterly toward the open waters of the Aegean. Melana, Joshua and Lydia, who had begun to waken, reversed and then resumed their late morning sleep. They returned to dreams fostered and furthered by the quietening rush-rush of the water from the departing storm.

Water, carrier; water, cleaver; water, cleanser.

Today, water would help allay hunger and slake thirst. Passover approached. Tonight, in preparation for Passover, Silas would join and lead other Bereans in commemoration. They would commemorate the events of more than 35 years earlier —events that had shattered the past; they would ponder happenings that shaped a future world from clastic shards of stone, slivers of a wooden cross and throbs of living water.

Water.... Silas reflected: Should he speak to the others about his dreams, visions and musings? Should he awaken them to talk about these matters? He mumbled quietly to himself, silently consoling his body, as he often did to aid digestion at the close of a meal. But there would be no meals today, and no other members of the household stirred with an ear to his musings; the family still slept, riding one last crest of the rain's lullaby.

Well, then, he would consider a brief instruction to himself: 'I could practice for a future time, a time when I might understand the nature of water and other created, voiceless substances. They do not strive.'

He would also counsel: 'Consider, just briefly imagine a part of the world totally without water —say, the zone of land that is now swamp — stretching afar, yonder, north of Berea. Take away water from that realm, and what do you have?

'Aha, I see your smile, Joshua!' He imagined his son's knowing smile. 'You foresee the end of the stenches of SummerTime, right? I agree; but also might not the usefulness of those glades come to an end as fishing places and homes for snakes?'

"'Not so fast!' Lydia would then exclaim. Oh, I can hear her say, "The snakes would go some place else," and Melana will correctly wonder if they would slither around our trees, infest the Triple River and increase the bother we already suffer from their kind?

'What else? Oh, you could no longer row through the reeds to Pella or Thessalonica. Reedy marsh would become barren, dry sand or caked mud. Nothing would grow. Old swamp would transform into a salt desert. Worse, if you started to walk into that zone, the drying air would crack your lips, wither your skin, and embrittle your hair. Ask me to stop describing my view of a world —a small world it would be, without water.'

Continuing, Silas revealed his insight of the past with a commentary: 'Our grandmother's grandmother knew God's presence in the waters. Water was one of the first things made from the clouds that blanketed earth during that forming time. I am convinced it is a pure creation, each particle nobly but simply framed, a substance of many unexplained properties. It is snow, ice, hail and rain; it can take on the clarity of air as well as the capacity to obscure the sun. Water conveys flavors in cooking, encases milled grains for shaping breads, and serves as the chariot for spirits in wine. Verily, and more.'

On this day, as the Passover season opened, water supplied additional virtues to the entire Berean family. Water, ceremonial wine, and small bits of unleavened bread provided their only food. It was their appetites' good fortune that most of them had awakened late, after the rain ended. Melana and Silas guided their neighbors through a day of preparations for the gathering at about sundown in the building Sopater had given for worship.

Neighbors volunteered: "Take these flowers for a bouquet." "Let us wash the windows." "We will bring folding stools for the elderly to sit on."

Melana took command of the arrangements so that all would be complete and on schedule. Silas carried skins of water, freshly taken from the spring. With Joshua in tow, Lydia and her brother took tubfuls from the banks of Triple River and carried that supply to the meeting hall. Eunice and Delphos arrived with slabs of unleavened bread; Aristarchus came with a cask of melon wine —"the best from the vineyard harvest of two years past," he claimed with a warm smile.

Just as all necessary articles had been put in place, the worshippers began to arrive —perhaps 40 families, a hundred or more people from Berea and its riverbank neighbors. Silas checked the room, making certain the group formed a set of concentric circles. Everything appeared ready for the commemorative prayers.

Suddenly, a commotion began near the entrance. Joshua rushed toward Silas, whispering loudly, "It's Caleb, Papa! Caleb and that… that… woman who lives with him! Can they come to this special service?"

Silas touched his son's head gently and walked toward Caleb and Zayda. Stopping in front of the couple, he directed them softly, "Come with me." The three moved to the places Joshua and Silas had planned to take; Silas took Caleb's hand and pulled lightly on Zayda's shoulder, inviting them, "Please join us here."

Silas stood in the middle of the room. "We shall now begin. Devote yourselves to quiet prayers —or simply watch and wait your turn while the foot bathing proceeds." Then turning to his son, he pronounced, "Joshua," and nodded; Joshua picked up two small jars of water and two cloths and walked to Caleb and Zayda. He caressed and washed Zayda's feet. Zayda, tensely watching, curled her toes and pulled her feet away, one at a time. Joshua, fearing to scorn, prayed to love this woman in a manner that could separate her brazenness from her self and soul. Similarly, he washed and wiped Caleb's feet, left and right, although Caleb displayed an active dislike for it: He snorted, spat, made a vomiting motion with his left index finger deep inside his mouth and a curling back of his lips. "You are our prize, aren't you?" Silas whispered loudly, resulting in Caleb's attempt to turn and pull his knees away. Nonetheless, Joshua continued and when he had finished, he nodded to them. With obvious reluctance, Zayda then sensed the pressure on her to do likewise, and she hurriedly washed the feet of the woman beside her; Caleb went hastily through the motions of washing the feet of the young lad beside him. Quietly and in that manner the entire gathering honored and imitated the action of the persons immediately next to them, washing the feet of the persons next in succession in the circles. The last to receive such loving were Silas and Joshua. Lydia washed her father's feet; Melana, her son's.

Silas stood. "Friends," he declared, "you have all been blessed more than I this evening, for only I have not washed another's feet. But I shall have proper due," he added smiling. "I may lead the prayers and help you break the first bread. Is that not enough?" "**Dayenu!** Yes, quite enough!"

his fellow worshiper shouted. They treated the wine to respectful dilutions with water and partook of the resulting combination by tearing and dipping fragments of bread into it. They sang and then marked times of silence, meditation or prayer —each as she or he could understand the significance of the time and embrace the space. Some chatting occurred, some quiet visiting.

At the close of the celebration, Silas issued another invitation: "In circles, my friends, let us face one another and seal compacts of peace with an embrace, a handshake, a kiss or quiet regard." Joshua gave Sopater's daughter a steady look; Melana exchanged a hug with Lydia.

Silas reached for Zayda's hand; she raised her fist and raged, "You are stupid sheep. This is all spit and goat's urine!" Then, in a wild obscenity, she raised her skirt above her nakedness and growled, "The deacon is going to lie with me some day, man to woman. Wait and watch. I am the spirit of happy harlotry in the new Rebels of Discord." Caleb nodded, raised his hands above his head and whooped in a frenzy.

Silas quickly stepped back from Zayda, signaled a kiss to Melana, and turned to the gathering. He boomed, "Good night! Peace and blessings to you all."

Later, back in the house, the family together spoke at length about what they knew of men and women —well-directed or misdirected, willing or unwilling to embrace steadying ways. "Such inheritances just do not wash away, do they?" Lydia observed for them all.

Very late, as he began to fall asleep in his wife's arms, Silas murmured, "I keep thinking of water in all its dimensions. It is a precious substance, seeming holy, in that it heads us toward connections we aim to make."

"Even the water of tears, love?" Melana inquired.

"Yes, tears too, flowing across closenesses. We must keep on visiting the well, asking for a drink, no matter whose bucket is dipped; always joining, cleansing and lessening thirst."

Melana whispered that she knew what he meant and offered sleepy accord, warmth and her touch. Silas fell asleep in a sheltering concentricity of baptism, spirit and water.

CHAPTER 12.

(A.D. 70) —WAR AGAINST JERUSALEM

\"Providence, even Almighty, does not reverse time or invert space, nor yet cancel the mysterious forces set to run between the earth, the clouds and the sun."—Epistle of Silas/

***

"No, Melana, I am not hungry this morning," Silas responded to his wife's question. She had inquired about sharing some ripe fruits and fresh breads as the day began. "Where did you send your good appetite?" she asked. "Come, tell me while I milk the goat...You do hear her bleating for my attention?"

They strolled to the east side of the house, moving around the currant bush that hid the downward path to the goat barn. As they walked, Silas took her free hand; with his own free hand, he stripped a few leaves from the bush. Rolling the leaves between his fingers, Silas confessed, speaking clearly, "Yes, my appetite appears to have left me. Perhaps it is darting about. More likely, it is hiding in Edhessa, which is where I ought to go. I ought to go to Edhessa for two or three days... on a mission of peace."

Melana had moved away from Silas and began to take a stool to commence milking, but Silas surprized her so that she almost tipped the stool. The nanny goat jerked her head as if she, too, were astonished. "A peace mission?" Melana repeated. "Is war promised, Silas? Would war occur here in Macedonia?" she asked, turning her head to look beyond the nanny's flank as she milked so that she might read her husband's eyes.

"I do foresee a war, Melanasha: Rome against my Jewish brethren at Jerusalem. About a dozen Roman officers have stirred up a recruiting campaign throughout these provinces, offering flashy uniforms and large bonuses —many *drachmae*, cartons of *denarii*."

Melana paused in her milking, as if to interrupt, but Silas continued, "You recall that Macedonian soldiers are widely known for their fighting skills—"

"And they are fierce," interrupted Joshua, who had joined his parents at the goat barn. Continuing, Joshua reminded them of his learning by shouting, "Silver Shields! The Romans call the warriors from our northern mountains Silver Shields!"

"Yes, Joshua, and the Roman recruiters want men who will help assure the destruction that Vespasian has decided to accomplish. I know some of those officers. I am going to try to persuade them to let my Macedonian friends stay steady in the fields with their crops and forego the sword." Silas looked out toward the mountains of Macedonia, far to the north; he would, he said, be off on his mission later in the day.

"Alone, Papa?" Joshua put the question quite directly. He and his parents began to walk back toward the house; he carried the container of goat's milk for Melana.

"I am never alone, son, but in this concern I hope to be joined by some other men. I will be looking for Lysimachus and Demetrios when I get into the region of Edhessa. They are persuasive speakers, themselves, persuasive enough, possibly, to blunt the blood-thirstiness that the Romans are trying to excite among the young men of the Macedonian mountains."

"You will go with the blessing of many," Dorcas inserted. She had just arrived at the little house. "Silas, I pray that you succeed. Success in that planned undertaking would reduce chances of Roman military action against my family. You do know that I still have hostages in Jerusalem?"

"Yes, Dorcas, but they are my hostages and Melana's, too, you realize," the deacon replied.

The group, centered on Melana, continued on toward the house, chatting. "Papa, sit with me while I drink a cup of warm milk. Will you do that?" Joshua asked as they re-entered the main room.

"Of course," said the Deacon, "and we may discover me nibbling off the little feast of figs, berries and breads Mother has laid out for you. You will allow that, I presume!"

Melana overheard and scolded Silas lightly, smiling as she asserted her willingness to prepare a full plate of food for him. "But, no, you had no appetite an hour ago; now you thieve a bit of this and a handful of that from your growing son!" She was teasing, was she not?

FEASTING WITH THE DEACON

Silas stared ahead as he bit into the breads; he looked out, as if across the horizon. Joshua now drew him back: "Are you off in a dreamland?"

Silas quickly came back, "No, Joshua, I am looking at God, over there in the spider's web."

"How do you see God there, Papa?"

"Look!" Silas commanded. "The web which was here was pulled and torn earlier today by Mother's goat. A marvel, the web seems; a miracle in the first place. It would be the pride of any planner, any Pythagorean expert in geometry. Join me; let's take a look at this marvel." Silas led Joshua to a closer inspection of the web in the nearby bush. "But this web seems even more nearly a representation of God in the spirit of a spider. I examined it carefully early this morning, apparently just after the goat had torn it while enjoying some currants. That was only a short time past, and the web was mostly tatters on one side, Joshua."

"Well, what now, Papa?"

"Now, it has been mended again. Not only mended, but the mending took up precisely on the torn ends, and the spider knew the formula for re-weaving it! Such power rests in intelligence, the wisdom of God in a spider; I will steadfastly pray that our fellow humans, fellow Romans —if you will —gain much wisdom by learning how to improve respect for life. Love of life: that is the true Wisdom. My loves, all of us can apply our gifts of intelligence to better ends than war."

Melana had changed to a flowered dress and had come to the place where they sat near the berry bush. "Silas, should you not be off to Edhessa? Joshua, you and I are going to visit the sick today. We will look forward to seeing Papa when he returns from Macedonia in a few days, right?"

And they all hugged, taking farewells. As he left, Silas looked in on his daughters, busy with some cooking and carpentry and ready to exchange love for his blessings. Lydia gave a hint of concern about her father's assignment; she spoke of his return in terms of important plans to 'sit down and look inside ourselves when you get back.' He nodded, smiling in agreement to the proposition. The entire household would hope for success in his efforts at Edhessa, maybe farther into Macedonia, as he strove to wage peace.

As Silas disappeared from sight down the trail, Joshua approached Melana: "Mother, Papa showed me the print of God in a spider web. Would there be such a sign in a bird's nest?" he asked.

"Certainly, son, birds' nests, peach seeds, snakes' tails, primrose petals and goat horns —to name a few other seats of signs," she assured him.

Silas spoke with Roman military officials at every crossroads and fortified camp. He carried his pleading and prayers north and west across the region, even east as far as Thessalonica. Regrettably, officers' bonuses and, indeed, their careers were greatly intermingled with the success of their recruiting —too much so to allow a mere deacon of a prospectively outlawed sect to dissuade them.

He then spoke and prayed with Lysimachus and other friends and sent hopes for a happy death for any warriors who would lose their lives in battle at Jerusalem; there was little else he could do. He headed back to Berea and reported on return that the motives of Roman emperors 'reflect the fact that there is a God who gave us free will, a will free to do right or wrong.'

"While I have been showing the rewards of peace and love and preaching that gospel of the Way Titus Vespasian marched Macedonian fighting men into camps near Jerusalem, launching a fierce and exhausting siege," he reported.

Melana asked if the siege may have harmed Silas's old friends there. "Yes, oh yes, my love.... Faithful Jews were killed by the hundreds, and Jerusalem-the-City destroyed and has ceased to be." Continuing, he reported that the surviving Sadducees and Pharisees were transported to Jamnia. He observed, without comment, that his former friend, benZakka, had assumed charge of the community. Word reaching Berea also told them that the Christian groups in Jerusalem fled to Jordanian Pella. The news drifted up from the port area of Thessalonica where many from Jerusalem had taken refuge, enabling Silas to learn some details of the sad news. When he made mental reviews of the reports, he recounted them, giving his interpretation of those events to his family. Bright-faced Lydia asked if God had left Israel. "Not at all," Silas asserted. "He is present there now, where He is desperately needed. Before time ends, God shall surround all that evil, enclosing it with love."

Lydia advanced her inquiry with a finger pointing at her own head. "Do I, Father, have a task there? Or am I just waiting for God to ship a saddle-bagful of love to the Roman Emperor?"

"Yes, husband, what do you think?" Melana inquired.

FEASTING WITH THE DEACON

"I will insist," Silas declared, "I do insist that each believer's duty is to be armed with love. It is the only irresistible weapon!"

MACEDONIANS WHO WARRED FAR OVER IN JERUSALEM

    Willows, weep! The barracks sleep, Blanketed in Roman trash —the rubble stands two-bodies deep;
    No trace of life can Rabbi borrow
    From Jewish barracks, deep in sorrow.   Willows, in the feeble rain, Let fall your leaves, to cushion pain.

CHAPTER 13.

(A.D. 71)—BOUND FOR MOUNT VERMION

(Melana is 48, Silas 63, Lydia 15)

\"Preserve life and keep its gifts as long as they bring you the prospect of happiness and the means of glorifying God."—Epistle of Silas/

Coming awake near dawn; those sounds...rain? Has it rained? Perhaps he should get up. Silas reminded himself: When hit from a rainstorm out of the southwest, this house leaks. Remember? Those manuscripts Titus and he worked over just last year —must not let them soak and weaken. Also, he promised Melana not to expose those lovely robes from Jerusalem to possible damage such as they escaped, almost miraculously, during last year's heavy floods. Better get up, and wasn't this the special day, anyway?

Silas moved, and Melana reached across the cot quickly, reached around him and whispered, "Don't you hear it?"

"Do you mean the rain?" he queried. "No, Love; someone is moving around in the kitchen."

They got up quietly and moved toward the curtain that separated the cooking area from the living and sleeping quarters.

No slippers; quietly now, they would catch and surprise the intruder, not overlooking the fact that the bold invader had several advantages over them. (Count the edge given by knowing the intentions —every raider knows about that advantage; the victim does not even know what to do when the invader does it. Add also that the invader dispatched her morning prayers to Heaven quite early, while it was yet dark. Supplement these power-packing conditions with the confidence that your victims love you and will appreciate what you have done, although they cannot see what she herself, the invader, is doing to make all that noise.)

Yes! This intruder held imposing advantages over that household; some she tucked in mischief behind her dark eyes; others hid inside ringlets of her black, glossy hair.

Suddenly, all the pans fell from the shelf, and Silas rushed into the kitchen, pushing through a thicket of pots. He next fought off a skilletful of ground meal and honey. As he turned the intruder to face him, she identified herself as "Just me, Lydia! Cooking something special; it is my birthday gift to you."

"Well, you are certainly the first person I ever knew who provided such a gift in a full range of sound, sights and stickiness!" commented her mother, laughing.

All three shared in the unexplainable mirth of chaos, and soon Lydia's sleepy-eyed brother and sister joined the activities that piled up near the cooking area. "Papa, you will be happy to learn that the rains did not leak on my head today," Joshua crowed.

"Yes, but Mother says heads are waterproof," Silas replied, tousling Josh's hair, as well as Johara's. "Our concern was for the robes and scrolls, which rain can damage," the Deacon asserted.

Lydia stepped forward, taking Silas's hands into hers. She turned her head from Joshua to Johara to Melana, looking into their eyes. Then she turned hard toward Silas, holding her gaze: "Papa, this is the day, remember?"

"For what, more rain, Lydia?"

"No, for the grand hike you promised me when I am 15 years old!"

"You did not hear me say we would hike up Vermion at the instant you fifteenth birthday arrived, did you?"

"But it has stopped raining already, see? See the rainbow over to the northwest? And I have been 15 for several hours! Also, Papa, I have decided on Vermion despite the fact that I have always wanted Olympos, the great mountain home of Zeus before the real God was known."

"Oh, I like that!" Melana remarked. "Spend all of your daughter's learning time in an effort to illustrate eternities, and she ends up forgetting the whole front end of time. You need another lesson, Lydia; perhaps your father can separate the *nevers* from the *forevers* for you.... But I do like the way you view the vacant Throne of Zeus out there, even as you substitute Vermion's broad range for the heights of Olympos."

FEASTING WITH THE DEACON

"I hear there are lions on Vermion," Silas commented. "We have no equipment for standing off such a beast, if he is hungry."

"I do not believe Vermion has lions or anything like that," Lydia replied, "and besides, he-lions are lazy; females, I hear, are the fierce hunters."

"Then we should stay clear and go to the lower mountains. To Vermion we should go only when we have planned it to the last possible detail, eh?" Silas declared.

Melana sensed that her husband was merely teasing Lydia, so she interjected, "Darling, you will be as well prepared today as you ever are. I can get a pack ready for you and Lydia in less than an hour after you eat the meal she claims to have planned. Lydia, what gathering of ingredients awaits your steady cooking hand from the odd remains on the floor?"

Lydia did not hesitate to claim her work: "Now that you ask, I want you all to know that I made my own birthday cake, Papa's recipe for a walnut cake with a special white wine and honey topping; if you help me clean up the mess, Dosh, you can have the first piece!"

"Lydia, you bargain on every transaction, don't you?" Silas challenged. "You made the mess; clean it up. Until you take care of that chore, not Joshua nor Johara nor Mother nor I will sample your cake or go further in arranging the hike up the mountain," he ordered.

"Of course, Papa; but may I feast on a birthday hug before I get out the scrubbing broom?" Silas embraced her tightly. "O-o—-ooh! That was a big hug. Anyone else?" Hugs went from Silas to Melana to Johara; when it came Joshua's turn, he chose to whack his big sister across her 'shapelies,' as he named her bottom-side.

"Son, that was not a fair hug, with the flat of your hand on your sister," Silas said in light rebuke. "You can make it up to her, however, avoiding a similar blow from me."

"How?" Joshua asked in hopeful relief.

"I would say she has taken care of it by quietly accepting your whack. So you are to help her clean up the mess she made, and when the two of you have finished, give her a good brotherly hug. And —"

"Papa! And what?" Joshua protested.

"And doing her chores while we are off to Vermion."

"Pretty high price for a bottom whack, right, Dosh?" Johara poked in.

"And, Johara," her mother said, "you will do your chores and the easy ones of Joshua's as well. We never know when you may need to step into another's sandals."

"Ekkkkh! Something really big, re-e-e-ally big, I guess, for a girl to be 15 years old!" Johara declared in mock admiration.

In the meantime, Josh and Lydia completed the cleanup, and the entire family met at a meal celebrating 15 years: as Melana said, "Fifteen years with Lydia did not seem much longer than 30 normal years."

They made a happy morning, feasting on life. It was mostly spent in steps to assure there would be enough food and bedding for the long climb Lydia would make with her father.

How long would they be gone? Oh, perhaps five days....
How far up the mountain would they go? Oh, probably to a height just below the pines....
How cold does it get there? Oh, perhaps cold enough to see frosty breath many a morning....

"Will you have to take all the food from here?" Lydia asked, somewhat teasingly.

"No," Silas replied, "we will find berries just getting ripe and some wild grapes on the northeast faces of the range. More important, and more tasty, the meadow-flavored honey we will likely find, to tear right out of the hive."

"Oh —Do we know how to do that?" Lydia challenged.

"Well, yes, I have harvested hive honey many times," Silas boasted, "and you, Lydia, may as well learn something useful on this hike, right?"

"Right, Papa, I am so thrilled about going! Can we start today?" Seeing an unmistakable mask move across his face, she knew, and confirmed it: "All right, tomorrow morning early?"

It was to be, but before darkness on Lydia's birthday, Silas stopped by Caleb's house. He suggested that Melana might appreciate Caleb's offer of any needed help while Silas and Lydia were away. Then, for the first time, Silas learned that Zayda no longer lived with Caleb. "No, she has left me; she claims our sense of values is not equal. After all this time! She tied up her belongings and marched away, saying our misfitness was destroying both of us. I think she robbed me of my money. She also took my tools and the old donkey, Deacon."

FEASTING WITH THE DEACON

Caleb looked toward the far horizon and then turned submissively to his caller. "I am alone, very lonely. And I am deeply grateful for any attention, Silas."

"Stopping to see Melana may be therapeutic for you, Caleb. Perhaps we should have a talk about the things that really matter when I return from this journey, this holiday with Lydia." Without enthusiasm, Caleb grunted an acceptance.

At dawn on the following day, Lydia and her father left for a holiday hike up steep paths and into heavy woods that clothed great Mount Vermion. Upward, pushing upward. If they were to camp for four nights, they needed to remain vigilant for firewood to warm them and to heat their food.

Thus, Silas suggested that they make a 'normative plan' (as the Romans would say) for the day:

First, plan tonight's stopping place.
Second, go there.
Third, survey the surroundings for firewood and obtain a supply.
Fourth, keep the firewood in a dry place.
Fifth, survey for safety, and prepare to lower that risk, if any.
Sixth, survey for food and prepare the amount that cooking calls for, placing it on high lift branches to move it beyond the reach of uninvited animal friends.

"Seventh, Papa, repeat the foregoing on the following days of the journey," Lydia advised.

"Quite good counsel, daughter," Silas acknowledged, "but the first day is merely to set the habit, not to impose an unchangeable pattern."

"I understand, Papa," she replied.

On the first afternoon, they moved around the rivers toward the far northeastern slope of Vermion and into elevations great enough to see slight changes in the variety of flowers. Removed a bit from the settlements of Berea, the medial slopes also furnished a larger population of wild animals: civet, fox and smaller animals —weasels and their kind. Nothing threatening, except the civet cats' imposition on the sense of smell.

Through the second night, they found wood to keep their fire burning, igniting it from their coals carrier; they had discovered wild berries and squash to stew, and they used the hard-braised lamb Melana had packed to furnish chewable food. "Keeps our teeth and gums healthy to have a tough piece of meat," Silas observed.

"Have you seen any lions or other interesting beasts?" Lydia asked on the third morning, as they faced into the higher elevations to the southwest.

"No, Lydia, I suspect any lions that use these grounds want to stay out of our range; probably none here."

That afternoon, however, they came upon an interesting find: a beehive, nicely connected to a swarm. "Stay back, Lydia," Silas warned. "Bees can be quite ferocious."

"So I have heard," she replied, "but how do we get a sample of honey to eat with the breads we have?"

"And to give us a small quantity to take back to Berea?" he asked.

"Yes, Papa, how?"

"First, we should build a rather good fire here, some distance from the hive. Now, we shall carry some of the burning limbs and some very damp, green wood over to the windward side of the hive. This will produce smoke, sufficient to quell them, to calm them while we take our quantity of honey."

Lydia watched carefully, as a diligent student. When Silas concluded that the smoke had dulled the bees, he took a sharp knife and sliced a handful of waxy material out of the top of the cone. With a continuous and deliberate motion, he moved farther and farther from the hive. When they were back by their campfire, Lydia gave him a probing look; he smiled and they both sat back on the log chosen to be their bench.

"Taste it; have some!" Silas insisted, offering her the honey. They both accepted their accomplishment with satisfaction.

"Papa, this is truly wonderful," Lydia pronounced. "What will we do tomorrow to give us a start back?"

"I suggest we go a little higher, to see the back side of the east-sloping precipices, then plan to move directly toward Berea." She agreed with her father's proposal, and they prepared for sleep on the third night.

Silas said, "I am going to take a short walk around to the spring and bathe before I retire. If you wish to bathe in the morning, I will help direct you to the place, Lydia."

"Marvelous!" she said and lay back, nestling among the bed clothing and leaves to search for sleep under the clear, starry sky.

FEASTING WITH THE DEACON

When Silas returned from the stream where he bathed, he said "Good night," and heard a muffled grunt as her reply.

"Well, daughter," he said to the entire night setting, "you seem to be getting healthful rest as well as a great holiday. This is another form of feasting, I say". The sky and her blanket signaled quiet infinities to him, and he slipped off into prayerful reveries and sleep.

In Berea, that evening, Joshua confided to his mother and Johara: "When I marry, I hope she is like Lydia." He looked west to the shadow of Mount Vermion and the imposing darkness of Mount Olympos far in the east, and Melana took his hand firmly. Johara pinched the back of his neck and chuckled.

CHAPTER 14.

DOWN, DOWN THE MOUNTAINSIDE

Sharply awake in dawn's crisp air, Silas stood, stretched and looked over toward Lydia. "Where is my breakfast?" he inquired. The tease did not arouse her, and his further inspection showed why.

An enormous monstrosity had visited his daughter. He jumped away. "Lydia!" he called and fell back as he saw the horror, the mutilation of her face and the ragged opening in her chest. "Dear God!" he cried, reaching for Lydia's body. In her right hand, she clutched a small portion of the honey comb. She barely breathed. He looked away; straightening up from her side, he looked carefully again. Across her neck and breasts ran the unmistakable marks, the deep claw tracks of a cave bear.

Silas picked up their bedding and tools, and he slowly wrapped Lydia in the thin blankets. He glanced along the slopes of the mountain, surveying the terrain that challenged him. It was really not possible to see Berea from where he stood. A terrible trip lay ahead. "I cannot carry her back to Berea in one day. I wonder if I can do the work in two days; perhaps I will fail in the effort. Well, if God so wills it, I shall have His hand. I will succeed...

"Perhaps Lydia will recover enough to help. No, she is too greatly wounded.... Even if we reach Berea, no healing physician could repair that young body. But I must not let Lydia realize how desperate her health has become; I must give her courage to make it reflect back to me. Perhaps a miracle, no, that is too much to ask; she is a miracle already."

Silas moved back, closer to Lydia's side; he confided, "Whatever we can do we will do it prayerfully, my love, and carefully, darling," he assured her.

Lydia could send only the faintest curl of a smile; her lips were swollen—her lower lip largely torn off. She continued to bleed badly. He wanted to tell her how it happened; he knew what had happened in the mauling, but would not allow himself to understand why. He could not accept her condition. The trip had begun with so many happy hopes!

He stepped away again to call out softly in a rambling prayer that mirrored his random rush; back and forth he moved, stumbling across the clearing, readying confusedly for the return to Berea:

"Lord, help me; help Melana and the others accept it. Help us; Lydia's body cannot long house her soul. How can she praise you? Help us, support me, heal Lydia!"

He raced back and forth on the mountain, frantic and harboring despair. He forgot how he had resolved to keep his concern from Lydia, and began to rage:

God! How could you wound me so deeply?

I have always praised You, and Lydia grew up with glories on her lips.

You, Almighty in your power, could have stopped the bear,

Directing its brutality elsewhere, else-times.

Why did you not do so? Why?

You could have held him back, or sent me a sign as I slept.

You have lost Lydia's means of prayer and praising You;

Why would You also risk losing my will to praise You —The strength of my faith now greatly endangered?

Hardly an echo answered him, but understanding arrived in two forms: First, an insight that the burden of sorrow would not exceed the family's capacity to love, and second, that the mutilation was merely a mark of the animal's bear-ness, his nature, and that alone, without malice. The mountain, then, silent.

Seeing now the sun climb the eastern sky, Silas felt the need for haste and lifted his daughter and a small cache of supplies. Holding her against his chest, he took off down the mountainside in a carefully crafted run, a stumbling run with knees wide apart. This gait soon overwhelmed him, and he drew up beside a pine tree where Lydia could rest while he regained his breath.

To Lydia he acknowledged, "You want to know how it happened, I am sure. Lydia, that was a bear, indeed, a bear that set on you in such a terrible way. It must have come for honey, its favorite treat. It was a cave bear; they do not eat flesh, but the bear, in its nature, attacked you simply because you held a small sample of good honey. I have put that rich honeycomb back into your hand; if you want to take a bit, please do. Hold on to life; hold the honey. Pray with me; send

> glories with me. I love you."

Lydia moved her gaze to meet her father's eyes; she whispered, "Praise God!" As they progressed, Lydia slipped out of consciousness and back into consciousness, each time weaker than the last, it seemed. Although losing strength, she had not lost spirit, and Silas perceived a glow and a countenance of song when she opened her eyes.

His arms ached. Perhaps it was only a dream, but his mind fashioned a carrier, it seemed. 'I see, in as sort of vision, a sled I could put together from branches, lashed with something like a rope.' Yes, the design was there, but the materials might be missing....

Something had to offer an alternative; both he and Lydia were chafed and sore from the hauling he had provided with his two arms.

He stopped; his endurance was failing, he knew. "Each time we travel shorter than the last." He left her, saying, "Lydia, I shall be away only momentarily." And he hurried to a thick shrub where he could pause in privacy by the large stone that stood adjacent. There, against the huge rock, and exhausted, he began again to rage and roar. The vilest of the bear's demons gushed from him. He moaned and whimpered. He clawed into the rocky mountainside. His fingers started to bleed. He lost control and momentarily lost faith. In that terror, he leaned against the stone and vomited.

After a while, he sensed a return of faith and began to formulate a new prayer, as it were, a litany of curses. Then he paused again, to regain his strength, for the silent prayer he sent reminded him that curses would not speed him toward Berea. He must find a way to bring Lydia to her mother's arms. To himself and God, he admitted that if he could not come to Berea, Melana would not know. So much, so very much Melana would not know.

He cried and vomited again. Then, he began to see the face of Paul before him, and he shouted to Paul for help; in deep sobs, he called for assistance from his friend, long ago put to death by Nero. "Paul," he demanded, "instruct an old deacon and scribe in the ways of tent-making and carpentry, as you knew them from Tarsus. I must have the help of some kind of vehicle to bear Lydia the rest of the way back to Berea."

In the silence he then allowed, he looked up and felt a strong glance as if visited by his old companion. At the close of that apparent visitation, Silas arose from the stone that stood near the thick shrub. He walked back beside his daughter. Lydia wriggled two fingers, ever so slightly, to signal affection to him, and Silas gave a gentle squeeze to those fingers. He saw that a small clump of honeycomb remained there and realized she offered it to him as she turned her wrist ever so feebly.

"Praise your Name, God, Sweet Giver of Life!" he sang. "Oh, how I wish Lydia's face were the vision and Paul's were solidly here. Even in my confusion, however, I know the cruel denial of that wish. The brutal truth is that Lydia's torn face represents the fact and forerunner of the loss we will soon suffer." Yet, still he sang.

Suddenly, two blackbirds flew at them, cawing and threatening, then four more dark-feathered birds. Silas took off his petasos to scatter them and drive them from the air, and he denounced their unwelcome presence. They retreated, and he watched the shadows of their dark flight fall back a bit. Then he took command of the situation again. "Well, I now know what to do to hurry us along, and we must do that," he reminded Lydia.

He began to construct a sled bed from two long branches and about a dozen short crossbar lengths taken from the nearby trees. He laid them out and tied some of the short pieces in place with strips torn from his own outer robe. Too soon he exhausted that supply. He looked for substitutes and realized he could tear strips of bark from the young green branches, and that those bark strings could be tied into place. He tried the sled with his own body as a test piece. As he rose from it he concluded that it needed to be made more rigid than the makeshift device he had wrought from a prayer and sticks. It would not last an hour without further reinforcement, he realized.

The birds—their feathers filthy-black, their cries threatening—came diving out of the sky again, and Silas rushed at them to shoo them away. They perched in a tree which stood a few yards away; they grew strangely quiet.

Quite overcome, Silas uttered a prayer of thanks for the birds' withdrawal and put a claim on a still unfulfilled need: "Praise again, Lord, but I am very short of time and require myself to be more completely clothed in wisdom. I need to know the way of tools and carpentry as does Caleb. Help my mind give fruit to that craft and my body, that strength."

FEASTING WITH THE DEACON

He glanced back at Lydia, and he looked closely at her hair.... Her long hair! He cut swatches of her hair with his hunting knife. He wove her hair into a sort of twine. In great haste now, he cut lengths of his daughter's hair, braiding and weaving it as rapidly as his fingers could move. Lydia peeked at him, her eyes feebly open. She appeared to whisper some phrase to him, and let her eyes close again.

"Dear God," he prayed again, "make these aging hands nimble enough for the task." He worked the braided hair ropes around the cross-bars at the ends of the sled bed, tying them tightly into place. But her hair would not tie tightly —would not remain a knot — so Silas once more required a skill he did not possess.

He took the unclotted blood that oozed from Lydia's wounds and transferred it onto the knots of her hair. Within a short time, his hands covered with clotting blood, he saw that the liquid of her life became transformed into a cement, developing into an agent of her last journey, as the knots became rigid enough for the sad purpose they served. Silas tested the joints of the sled, and was calmed by the tough strength they displayed. They would suffice, he trusted.

A stillness ruled, but it puzzled Silas. Out of the stillness on Vermion's cruel slopes, an abrupt fluttering of wings broke the silence. Silas looked up to see a white dove enter the flock of black birds which remained on the perch. Quite as suddenly as the dove's arrival, the six black birds seemed to dissolve and disappear, transforming to white doves. Thus, the single dove became a flock of seven doves, all white, who also took wing. As they flew up from the tree where the demons had perched, Silas noticed that one dove bore a patch of blood redness at its throat.

Now, a return to the task at hand. He lifted his daughter into place, easing Lydia into position on the sled and securing her to it with the last free strips of his own clothing. "We resume our lumbering pace, Lovely Child!" he announced.

After another half day of the trip, when he felt assured that he could endure and Lydia might also remain alive that long, he told the mountain, "This scars all of us, but is only one battle. We have not lost."

There came a passage of dreams, haunting visions, then a faint humming; "What do I hear?" Silas asked. "Oh, Lydia, that old ditty? You hum one line, and I shall sing the next." Thus they continued for a while as he and she tried to chant and repeat 'Flower on the Mountain', the lovely song he had composed on coming to Corinth some 20 years earlier.

Shuffling from exhaustion, Silas carried Lydia into Berea the following afternoon, who-knew-how-many days after she had been mauled by the bear. Neighbors met Silas, and then they ran to tell Melana. All groaned in their sympathetic sadness at the sight of Lydia, torn and bleeding. "How can she recover?" "How did it happen?" "How can Melana and Silas accept this catastrophe?" "In that state, how can Lydia not die? What if she dies?"'

To every question, every questioner, Silas gave the same reply: "Trust in the goodness of God; pray for the peaceful repose of her soul; all will be well."

Melana came running, falling to her knees in front of Silas. She rose, weeping. She lifted Lydia's body from Silas' aching arms.

Slowly, the mother lowered her daughter to the ground near their house —the house where Lydia had been conceived and born. "Precious Lord," she prayed, "take this soul home. The body has been greatly destroyed, and we cannot repair it in Berea."

When it was obvious that Lydia no longer lived, Joshua and Silas knelt with Melana and they all wept. Their cries tore the village air, and their moans troubled the streets of Berea. Sabaka, Lydia's dog, now growing old, approached and then drew away whimpering, with his muzzle between his front paws.

Johara saw and heard, and walked over to the doorway. Peering in, the five-year old saw Skepsi, the family cat. Johara carried Skepsi back to the spot where Sabaka grieved. Softly stroking both pets, she announced to them, "Skepsi, Sabaka: My big sister just died."

\"Glorify God when you suffer deepest loss; when abandoned; when thieves have taken your goods."—Epistle of Silas/

CHAPTER 15.

STILL FARTHER DOWN

By the end of" time, God's love shall transform even Satan, overcoming all evil."—Epistle of Silas

On a hazy morning, a day after her death, the community buried Lydia. Caleb came; many other neighbors joined in honoring her memory. Hymns and flowers decorated Berea that day. Yes, even the air of Berea was decorated by the words of many who loved her, who had watched Lydia reach and search for the ways of charity, paths to joyous service. Coming up from the burial, Silas left his family briefly to visit the nearest hive of bees, which inhabited the great meadow. He stood beneath the sturdy shrub that supported the huge hive, and he proceeded to inform the bees about the future absence of Lydia, who had often come by the honey bower with her parents.

The ritual of telling these bees near the place where she died was his own private ceremony. He came to their kind, knowing that this hive was not the source of the honeycomb on the mountain. However, he trusted neighborhood bees to tell those on Mount Vermion, and the silence in the Berean meadow seemed to confirm his trust.

As he completed his return from the burial place on the hillside, Silas encountered Caleb, who pulled at him, holding him off the roadway as if to impart great news. "While you were away," Caleb muttered, "Melana and I made love. Twice, Silas. I finally understand my longing for her. Her body is beautiful." He smirked and giggled, and started to skip away.

Silas would not permit Caleb to escape this time. He lunged at the offender, grabbed his elbow and pulled him back, then struck him hard with his right fist on the side of his cheek and jaw with such force that teeth spewed from Caleb's mouth.

Silas picked up two of Caleb's teeth from the ground and threw out a denial. "Caleb, you know you lie!" Silas declared in hot anger, restraining himself firmly. "I am certain you lie with as much stain on your hurtful words as we see on these teeth. Still, I do not know why you choose to hurt. It will not work here, because I do not believe you. Even if Melana told me that you and she shared a bed, I would still love her, and love her absolutely."

It seemed that Caleb would answer through the bloody froth at his lips, but he gave only sullen looks to the deacon, so Silas continued. "Many, many errors, a multitude of wrongful thoughts infest your mind, Caleb. They require our prayerful attention soon, and I shall help you try to cleanse your mind, if possible. Your filthy mind."

Caleb stood and looked down at the path, then spat through his wounded toothlessness toward Silas. The deacon paused, closed his eyes briefly, then spoke even more softly. "Whatever be the outcome of that attempt, Caleb, in the calibrations of time, you have set a low and sorry standard: No day can ever out-do this day as a time of sadness."

Silas turned to look straight into Caleb's eyes; he lifted his hands, grasped both of Caleb's thin shoulders and declared, "Caleb, you can yet believe me when I tell you I love you. Even amid the madness you have carted into this village to dump upon its sorrow and our mourning for Lydia, I can foresee peace and more miracles of love. I wish you could do so, too."

Caleb's eyes blazed and he seemed unable to control his body; he trembled and shouted, "Oh close your mouth, Silas! You sound like an unseasoned child. Stop this forever chattering about love and happiness, Silas; put your trust in power," Caleb yelled through bloody lips. "Live among the pleasures power can bring. Stop masquerading foolishness as the fruit of faith. Surely you know better. We Rebels of Discord know otherwise and will dispatch all of you who preach peace and forgiveness. So, stop it, you fool."

"Indeed, I shall not stop," Silas promised. "This is the Way," he asserted. "Now, Caleb, go with God. Examine your thoughts and mend your manner."

Caleb shouted back, "I have no need to do that and can tell you that I have always felt comfortable with my actions without following your suggestions. I have no need of them."

"Caleb," Silas began, "if you do not perform an examination of the interior of your mind, you will not likely mend your ways. You will be doomed to feel shut out, unhappy, mean and lost. I wish you could realize how much happiness is within reach if you would simply reason and repent a little." Caleb merely shrugged and scratched his anatomy in the same obscene gesture he had brought to Berea some years ago. Silas made a friend's salute, facing Caleb, and then watched as Caleb turned away.

Separating from Caleb, Silas walked across a clearing to the place where his family stood waiting in the shade of a clump of trees. He touched them and hugged them one by one, and all together they hugged him. One breath, one spirit encircled them all as Silas bent down and reached for Johara. He took Johara into his arms and walked between Melana and Josh back up to the house near the spring.

Caleb shuffled down the hillside, disappearing in the dust....

Taking Josh aside, Silas asked him to go out among the woods and find some four tusks that might have dropped from a wild boar. "You may discover that your friends will want to help you in your hunt. When you have found the tusks, please take them to your mother. I shall ask her assistance with the next step. My appreciation, Joshua, and to all your helpers."

Some time later, Melana came to Silas with a report that "Joshua has given me four tusks of wild boars, saying that you want to do something with them, right?"

Silas then went with Melana to their parlor, alone. They spoke in soft voices for some time, following which they told Joshua and Johara that they would be gone and back in less than two hours. During that time, Silas rounded up and commissioned a local healer artisan who also went along to Caleb's home, and who arranged for the group to meet with Caleb there.

Melana took charge for her family, speaking from his doorway: "Caleb, we are here to offer a mouth for your future use and appearance. If you will accept the repair we have brought a specialist, an artisan who learned the newest craft on Kos, where they re-make the mouths of wounded soldiers."

"I am not a wounded soldier and do not take kindly to the form of this offering. It comes from the peace-preaching deacon who has attacked me for no cause, no cause, Melana! But, what do you have?"

Melana spoke slowly to emphasize the importance of the assistance they offered. "We have some new-found teeth made by our friend from Kos, and he has shaped a frame from bone and shellac to hold those teeth in place in your mouth."

"What?! You would bring a stranger, one who accompanies Silas, my enemy, to my door and suggest that he should rebuild my mouth with wood and lac and recovered teeth? Never!"

Melana's softly voiced comment gave all the others pause: "As I understand it, the work that this craftsman from Kos has proposed to insert inside your mouth will not serve well when you eat but will make you look even more handsome than you have in the past. You may wish to take it out at mealtimes, perhaps —after you have drawn some believing woman to trust you and attend to your spiritual needs."

Caleb shot a gap-toothed grin at the others and moved aggressively toward Melana, who blocked his progress as he said, "I always knew you would be my salvation. This proves it, Melana."

Pulling back farther, she said, "Salvation is not the word, Caleb. We will leave you in the skilled hands of Jered, this man from Kos. Best to you and may blessings fall to all of us: You with new teeth, and we with new hopes for you."

Melana, Josh and Silas stood respectfully, made their farewell and moved away, taking the path back to their home to rejoin Johara and continue their ceremonies of bereavement.

MOURNING FOR LYDIA, (by 'Dosh', her brother)
Andros brings a Lydian rose: Young love's fevers fade;
Mother comforts us and Papa.
Neighbors stop to pray; Sister! Daughter! All are wounded.
All the village weeps.
Waters flowing down the mountain
Be its tears of grief.

RECOVERING

Heavy sobs I hear throughout this wounded house,
but loudest in her sleeping room;
We cry now, and survey for far horizons still to loom. Those futures
—each may bear its charge of sadness, grief and sorrow;

FEASTING WITH THE DEACON

But joys both near and far can outweigh tears, And I shall match each joy with jeweled cheers.

All will be well, all well again, at dawn tomorrow.

CHAPTER 16.

STILL DEBATING PAUL: ADVERSARY'S PASSAGE

"God, who is perfect, cannot suffer from any wound we intend to transmit."—Epistle of Silas/

***

Lydia had been buried three years ago. Zayda, less missed, little grieved, had been absent as long. With no claim to have become a believer or a follower of the Way, Caleb appeared to have become more caring and thoughtful, appeared to be less scheming. "It seems to me that he does not tell lies as much as he used to do," Joshua volunteered one morning.

Whatever the change, to whatever degree it materialized, almost everyone accepted that the change had resulted in large part from Caleb's cooperation with the prayerful resolve of Deacon Silas. But not everyone agreed that a constitutional change had occurred, or —if it had —that it had been accompanied by timely and sufficient signs of remorse and spiritual repair.

Many from outlying villages held an indelible, unforgiving grudge in their accounts with Caleb. Among their other grievances against him, Macedonian hill people did not forget the inferior and overpriced cabinetry he had delivered to them, one-by-one, over the years.

"Naturally, I am not proud of everything I have sold, but I am no longer in business of making and doing," Caleb had said. Continuing to excuse himself, he added "I now think and meditate on higher things!"

Several former customers, once swindled, did not accept his claim, and asserted that Berea deserved to be rid of the condition they called 'Calebosis'. Among those who felt the lasting sting of his injuries were some who threatened to cure the disorder they named, saying they knew of ways harm might befall him on certain roads. Caleb always drew back out of earshot when these sayings against him were voiced, but villagers in general seemed to take the noisy threats seriously.

Although Silas warned Caleb that "You ought to make some effort at restitution for your shoddy products and cheating," none was offered. Caleb did not take such action.

"I'll stand by my previous statement," he said. "Let them call me stiff necked and stubborn. I know my soul and will not make any public apology."

Andrus and his cousin thus stumbled across a badly beaten Caleb on the upper path one afternoon. He was near death, perhaps dying, from cuts and pummeling. A gash on his left leg looked as if it went dangerously near the bone.

Conveyed back to Berea, Caleb was taken to a room in the meeting place where injured and ill strangers were commonly housed and fed. Silas, upon being called to visit the beating victim, brought Caleb's favorite sweet cakes and stayed with him, abiding in vigil over many weeks.

After a long convalescence, Caleb showed only a festering leg sore to worry Silas. Adding to the signs of recovery, Caleb began to make remarks tinged with sharpness, such as, "My death, at long last, might have been a welcome event, most welcome for Silas, right?"

"No," replied Berea's sturdy deacon. "I am delighted and grateful for your apparent recovery, having prayed so earnestly for it." Silas continued, telling Caleb, "I would not want to let you go so easily, too cleverly avoiding debates about difficulties on our journey to God. Caleb, you and I both hunger for these rough games. They spark our spiritual travel; banter, well-meant, can strengthen our belief as we go up and down the little pathways of faith. For me, at least, it assures a more open acceptance of good."

"Am I now officially Paul's replacement in your arguments, your endless search for something to ponder, and someone who —in the end —will disagree with you about your soul's own journey?" Caleb inquired noisily, propping himself on an elbow. He winked at Johara, who had accompanied her father that day.

"Do I provoke such a quarrelsome clatter, Caleb?" Silas asked. "For a certainty, you and I are not yet finished, but you are certainly not Paul's replacement. Recall, if you will, that my late companion was bald, whereas your shaggy hair still covers your lean face and now turns white, and —"

"You know, Silas," interrupted Caleb, "I believe Johara genuinely appreciates our loud discussions," Caleb said as he watched a bright smile widen across her face. (She had reminded many of her sister, now buried on the hillside. However, to their separate credits, both Caleb and Silas had demonstrated to her that she represented no one but herself.)

"What I really appreciate is that you seem likely to be well again, Caleb", Johara declared. "I also want you to be the first person outside the family to know that I have decided to become a missionary."

"Outstanding! You will do well; you will not mind defining the truth. Your father still avoids that discussion with me."

"I have only suggested that we will do better asking for examples than definitions, Johara. Definitions confine; and to some extent, they actually destroy meaning," Silas declared. He broke a small stick he was holding; that seemingly unconscious act embellished his assertion. "That is my outlook."

"How is that outlook, Papa?" demanded Johara. "I understand differently from the scriptures. Some of Paul's writings convince me that definitions offer standards and codes of conduct. They help the beginner—"...

"—Remain a beginner, Johara? Caleb admires definitions because he loves to quarrel with me, as Paul did," said Silas, as if to reprimand both of his hearers. "And, Caleb, I have always felt that your approach was to bait me with tiny fragments of the law while we ought to explore the doings of the spirit."

"Are you bringing up the past to me, Silas?"

"No, Rebel Asimios, 'silver haired Rebel': We can let the past lie still while you hair turns whiter and whiter," Silas told him.

Caleb winced; clearly, he did not welcome the name Silas called him. Twisting, he looked at Johara as if to ask if she knew where the label 'silver-lad' came from.

"Yes," Johara admitted, "I, too, have been silently calling you that, Caleb. Asimios, 'silver one'; do you approve the new name?" she asked.

"Sounds fitting to me, as I age and observe the snowy silver tops of the mountains each winter. Meantime, your father loses more hair and—"

"Caleb, quite enough!" boomed the deacon, foreseeing a tease. He touched his head, near bald under his petasos. It seemed a sign of shyness. "See, some truths change. Others do not!" Silas insisted. "When we know the truth, our minds match perfectly with it, even if the truth appeared to perish once on a battlefield."

"Or, Golgotha Hill, Silas?" Caleb inserted.

"Caleb, I do not like that comment," Johara said.

"Well, let us try some other subject. Oh—heh—that was a nasty pain, there in my insides, not too good," Caleb jerked his body and fell back on the pillow in a weak spasm.

Silas came to his side with a cup of water. "Can we make you comfortable, friend?" "Yes: Tell us the story of the olive trees, Silas." Silas looked at him in some uncertainty. Caleb repeated his request, "Go to the story of the olive trees, Silas. That will help, because it will invite my mind to another concern."

"Papa, I have never heard the story of the olive trees," Johara remarked. "Neither have I," added Joshua, who had joined the trio in the hall. "Neither has Caleb!" shouted Silas. "It was mentioned once; Mother and I were listing parables we might tell. We were inventing parables that Jesus and other masters might have overlooked."

"Proceed, please," Caleb urged. "It may help me see some message, some part of the gospel in a convincing light."

"That last remark troubles us a bit, Caleb, but I will stick to my brief story. It criticizes the common practice of casting barren olive trees into the fire. It is a wasteful practice, and even an unwise act, contrary to our love of a living thing.

"I proceed: First, take note that olives do not bear fruit unvaryingly from year to year. They start late, only after several years' care. Even when they have borne good harvest, they may not do so again for three more years. Yet their fruits are so rich-spirited, so nutritious!"

"Is that the end of the story?" Joshua asked.

"No," replied his father. "You should also learn that olive trees, grown from seed, do not produce fruit abundantly. They may be barren, as a matter of fact. How, then, you ask? When you watch olive keepers carefully, you will find that they graft twigs of seedlings to sturdy stock, seasoned and strong. The young send forth new branches, prolific. Their fruits are so delicious!"

"Is there more?" Caleb asked. "Your story bothers me, since it does not tell me what it tells me. However, keep it going. My side pains have grown unbearable; help me put my mind on something else."

"There is a little more, yes. Observe that olive trees make the mountainside unfit for other plants. Why? The olive possesses only one root, which anchors the olive tree in its own fashion but spoils the possible placement for crops and other trees. The mountainside becomes bare, yet we accept its stark nakedness as the price of an olive grove. We accept it because olive fruits are precious and so essential to our needs and tastes."

Then Silas paused, and came closer to Caleb, as if to find a new way to comfort him. He attempted to take Caleb's hand, but the bedfast man pulled away impatiently.

"Is that all?" Caleb asked. "That was not even a story, Silas! Furthermore, my former neighbors on the east slope, they graft old olive twigs on healthy young roots."

"Yes, Caleb, I am familiar with that practice, too. It does not promise a yield every year, and it tends to produce small olives, monotonously small fruit. We are in an orchard that calls for us to try ways that induce variety.…. You know what I mean —all of you." "Not only do we know what you mean, Father," Johara said. "We have also sacrificed our admiration for the beauty of olives, the tastiness they add to our cookery and the poetry of their treeness for the overwhelming details you have offered. Really, it pains me to lose an opportunity to appreciate olive groves as the price for scrutiny of some minute aspect of horticulture."

Silas smiled resignedly, but Caleb swore at the deacon in agreement with Johara, adding, "You have made my pain come back! It has grown worse. You wanted it that way! You have always hated me, Silas."

Josh and Johara gave their father a sign that asked if they should leave, but Silas motioned , 'No', that they should stay. He hoped that all three would see a revolt of his spirit, a somersault of the soul. He foresaw the end but hoped that Caleb might be drawn to repent before that end, repent and set aside wrongs, capture good. Silas prayed it would occur if God's will.

Instead, Caleb raved, "You always thought I schemed to make mischief and lie. Always! I could have been a good man, a truthful man, if you had believed in me, Silas. Silas, you horrible pretender, you have caused all of my misfortune since you came here to Berea. I was doing well until you came."

Silas spoke with soft strength, "Caleb, forgive me for any wrong I have done to you." He urged that it was time —perhaps the last available time —for Caleb to join in the prayerful walk with God. "Joshua and Johara will accompany us, I am sure," he added, taking a cue from the sober nods his children gave him.

Caleb retorted, "See! You come forth at this time with honey on your tongue because you want your son and your daughter to think you have done me no wrong. Well, children, it is a cute and vain trick. Do not believe him. Your father has hated me ever since I told him about your mother and me."

Out of their innocence, Johara and Josh simply looked at Silas, who reached and held them in a strong embrace. He looked back at the patched-up man on the mattress; he closed his eyes; he remembered many things and heard Caleb in a choked whisper. Caleb was fighting to gain the power to speak through his torn lips that showed his wounds when he wore his special mouthpiece. Even when he put it into place, he spoke with great difficulty; he appeared to struggle for breath. Observing that condition, Silas paused in his prayers to say, "Caleb, you know that I have never hated you. You also know that Joshua and Johara are not to interpret evil of any sort from your reference to Melana. It is a lie."

"Yes, yes," Caleb looked away, then looked back at all of them, each of them, weakly confiding, "You say I lie.... Do you know, I have always lied? I do not know why, but I have always lied, and am probably lying as I speak now. I taught the lying Cretans to lie; I lied to Zayda, even as she rested in my arms, lied to my closest friends, to everyone. Lied when I confessed the Lord, that I was converted to the faith of love, the Way of your master...." He paused to press and comfort his agony.

"Oooh! Such pain. One more pain like that one, one more sting of death.... It nips my heart, makes me recall the high flight of loving a woman. O-ooh. Come close, Deacon; I die."

Ahead of her father, Johara rushed to Caleb's bed. "Asimios, do you die? I pray for you and your eternal soul, Asimios. Do you die, Simi? Oh no!"

"No, I lied. I even lied about lying, as now, I lie. In truth, I live, Johara...." He took a deep breath, raised a bit on the cot, and rested into Johara's embrace. Then he moaned, reached to stroke his prurient crotch and fell back, dead. Dead Caleb, dead Chief of the Rebel Neo-Shuthalhites.

All of the family realized that he was gone; they felt the departure of darkness as if an evil had removed itself and the opportunity to be healed by love.

"How very much I had hoped to accompany him in the walks, talks and debates, to go with him in joy on the journey to God," Joshua lamented.

FEASTING WITH THE DEACON

"Yes, I, too," Silas asserted. "Caleb did not seem to understand that we had been ready for many years to join him or help him get started on that walk. But in planning our own journeys and assisting other Bereans on theirs, we gave too little time to him. He did not accept our love; he fought our attempts to give him merest samples."

"I think Old Simi always listened suspiciously for evil's approach and for an opportunity to capture it," Johara declared with a grin. She added, "He could imagine he heard wrongs charging toward him from every direction."

Her father softly observed, "Satan marches silently, with boots that never squeak. It appears that Caleb never got around to listening for the parade of good things. He never drove the Old Devil away; he courted the evils that hung around, and then he blamed his friends for the consequences...."

They were quiet together for some time longer; then Silas acknowledged the need to resume the work of Berea. "Let us go; we should make arrangements for a funeral tomorrow," he suggested. "I want to give our whole church an opportunity to compose a proper prayer and arrange a prompt burial for this neighbor who struggled through life."

"First, Papa, I want to tell Mother how hard he tried," Johara requested. Silas stayed with the clay of Caleb while Johara and Joshua ran on toward the little house behind the wide gate.

CALEB: PASSAGE IN PAIN

This wound, not visible,
can yield no blood to staunch;
This inchoate cut
from all those stabbings I have pressed against
Whichever way I moved. But I must move.
Must move, and thus must lacerate myself
in any enterprise I launch.

Life's End

'... each feels crushed in darkness 'neath the weight Of all the world. There chaos reigns;

All things the sun beholds, in rising and in setting,

Grow but to decay.

Life is but practicing for death;

Though thou be slow in coming, still

LEONARD BARRY BARRINGTON

We hasten of ourselves. The hour
which gave us life begins our death.'
—Seneca, 65 CE
[committed suicide by royal (Neronic) order...]

CHAPTER 17.

(Year 79 A.D.) —DISCOURSE AND PROPHECY

Looking beyond \"It is acceptable to God that we admit confusion over little absurdities."—Epistle of Silas/

"Papa, you and I do not need a large meal this evening, do we?" Johara suggested, excusing her desire to continue the chat Silas had begun that morning.

Today, and for the past few days, it was just the two of them at the house. Melana and Joshua had gone to northern Macedonia, visiting the communities and churches west of Edhessa. They planned a week's work before returning to Berea, a week to be devoted to feeding and singing among those foothill villages. Silas and Johara had spent those days cultivating the spirit at the three little chapels and the main mission church in Berea. In addition, they found time to engage in lively chats and quiet conversations as they weeded their diverse gardens.

Silas had said earlier, "I am much more dedicated to the growth of these missions and the fruit of good works than I am concerned about getting rid of the weediness in the spiritual fields of Macedonia. Understand?"

Johara declared, "This talk about a form of supportive gardening is interesting but not accurate enough to tell unbelievers the direction for right living. In fact, Papa, I do not support parables as much as you do. Just stay with the lesson and stick with the facts, and let comparisons go.

"Are you saying that you don't want to use examples to instruct the mysteries?" her father asked.

"Exactly. Papa, there are no examples of truth, except that nothing compares well. Each idea has to stand and anchor in its own goodness. There are no examples of paradise except the glorified resting place of the soul. It is not like a mustard seed, despite that parabolic story told by the Master, Himself. It is like nothing else, and the same applies to other spiritual realities, I think." She stopped, as if her earnestness had proved her right, and brought her to imply that she could now rest her case, as she argued, "I think the examples of the good life may be exceptions, and we need to look at the lives that most of us pass. Nothing exceptional in the way we deal with one another in this house, is there? Also, if we are to look at the people who call themselves saints, we see that we could hardly duplicate their lives."

Johara hardly stopped for breath as she continued to lecture her father, saying, "We have only a cycle of days and a rather tedious set of chores to glorify, and I have long cherished the fact that you and Mother do just that. No clouds parting, nothing that I could not do. But to put the matter to a test, how could a virtuous and vigorous girl in this neighborhood become a virgin mother? Yet that once-in-an-infinity Mother of Jesus is to be our model. How? and how can my friends or I copy her?"

Silas took a long time to reply but finally said, "I understand the truth of your words, and I have always avoided any move that would seem to put the apostles on pedestals. Pedestals crack and give way; they are so fragile. Instead, I would ask that we live in simplicity, in honesty, dealing in fairness, asking no special favors, doing no harm. Yes. But it is difficult to convert what I have just said into a teaching lesson, most difficult."

"Papa," Johara murmured, "I shall just try to find illustrations in the lives of young children and in the nurturing ways of those who take care of others in hospices or homes for the sick. I want to be sure that I put a leash on my zeal so that is does not race ahead of my understanding."

Silas reached for his daughter's hand, saying "You have gained Wisdom, the truest wisdom of the Way, and we can be certain of the banquet from that Feast." They embraced.

Earlier in the day, as they worked the herb garden together, Silas had started them into a new discourse. Taking up Johara's point about people who try to put God on the spot, Silas had advised her, "You will always have to counsel against prayers that forever ask for favors —some require specific favors by a certain date! Continuously, you will have to urge their search for openings to serve and praise. Your own manner of living will constantly remind them that the life of the spirit outshines the importance of celebrating festivals or calculating coincidences with moons and eclipses."

FEASTING WITH THE DEACON

Johara had been turning that comment over in her mind and hoping to avoid the need for going back to a hot cooking stove. She hoped Silas' desire to continue the conversation would prevail over his normal appetite for a large meal. With two turns of logic in his reply, Silas smilingly ravaged that hope: "Daughter, you must be mindful of the needs of your flock, even if it consists of but one aging sheep. He, too, even your aging parent, requires feeding. Feed the temple of my soul, sweet child."

But Johara was not overcome so easily as her hopes and responded with a noticeable weariness, "I am sometimes too weathered, too abraded and unraveled, to be sweet, Papa. I may have to harden myself against various impulses and attitudes as the years pass."

"Johara, dearest, you will not have to become hardened. Become softer yet, keeping your mind fast on its goal.... You have unusual gifts, indeed, in that you still seek wisdom while embracing the flock that comes to learn from you. I saw; I saw that last week by the warm waters of the gulf, witnessing the great reach of your dark brown eyes. Your people love your songs, your skills in giving to their spiritual needs.... As well, your cooking skills."

He paused long enough to recapture her attention. As Silas continued, he added an orator's tone to his voice and, teasing, caught her brown-eyed glance in his: "Sometimes they need a large meal, a generous feeding to combat fierce appetites just at the moment you have least time to pare the vegetables and grind the wheat. For some of us hungry ones the gift of prophecy helps; for others, we count on a charitable giver's keen vision and well-calibrated ear to combine and sense unexpressed yearnings."

Realizing he had caught and trapped her vulnerability to odd humor, Silas went on. "Yet, with all my talents, I seem unable to prophesy how many moons will wax and wane before I enjoy a meal from your hands again!"

"I know you may be teasing me, Father Silas, but watch me now! I shall prepare a somewhat more substantial meal than I had planned; it will keep for a second day, and Mother will not return with Joshua from Edhessa until tomorrow night, correct?"

"We will tell them to speak very well of the product of your efforts, won't we?"

"Papa, you are a treasure! Now, what guidance about the calendar can you give me? Or does the idea of calendar go farther than measuring moons? I suspect you do not use a measure for time; you simply sense time and timing, I believe."

"Yes, I know this family, Johara. We will probably allocate and ladle time in various ways, but they will be ways quite beyond measuring moons and seasons. Certainly, I know none of us will require time to include all the little invented ceremonies calling for God to come along with schemes aimed to our personal benefit."

"Such as?"

"Well, such as making a hobby of shrines. No one can forge a new spirit by simply visiting the site where Stephen was stoned or where Paul's head fell away on the rocks in Rome. Teach your disciples to frame attitudes of service; they ought to bring fully formed devotion along wherever they go. Then they will always be ready to honor places set aside for worship."

"Do you say that it is entirely in attitude and intention, Papa? Surely not!"

"Oh, let them bring intentions, to materialize in deeds. Encourage your friends to offer dancing and singing as services to others and to the GodHead. We should skip, play the harp and beat drums for others and for the glory of God. We may, Johara, now listen! We may also cook for others, feeding their bodies' needs. By such simple service, we may reflect the soft hearts of children, as we should all aim to become again.

"Children!" he added with some strength, "children do not require the calendar to work magic, as some of my aging friends (and your aging friends) ——as some do."

"Oh yes, we do, Papa. They do! Papa! Remember, tomorrow! Tomorrow! When they wake up tomorrow, everything wonderful is to happen on some marked day, you know."

"Yes, Johara. That would make tomorrow the most important day that God ever gave us. But marked days do not result from moons and planets falling into certain paths and patterns in the sky."

"Do you not join us in celebrating the seasons? Papa, do I need to remind you that you taught us to commemorate anniversaries, transfigurations and births? No, you know very well we take joy from such celebrations."

"Johara." Silas saw he had exaggerated his case, but he wanted to retain the point of his reply. "Johara, stay mindful of the lesson I am trying to teach: Our spiritual exercises ought to avoid mechanical routines; they should actually punctuate our lives. Certainly, I need to observe dates, recalling some events: my coming to Berea first, meeting and marrying Mother, your births, Lydia's death, the time of Jerusalem's fall, even the day we found Skepsi-cat-kitten in the rain."

Johara finally began to select and set up her preparations for the meal, but she appeared also compelled to catch her father's wisdom and love while they flowed.

"Papa, you have a gift for looking to the shape of things in the years ahead; what do you see?"

"The future is pretty clear, Johara. I do not mean that we know the names of empires, kings, saints or scoundrels for a thousand years ahead —

"But I can foresee grandchildren's grandchildren's grandchildren who will want to explain why certain trivial events occurred. They will mark the calendar with colors, signs and symbols. They will construct a form and expect others to practice it within some location, some remembered place. For the sake of ceremony alone, they will compel their associates to fit a recipe at a specified time."

"Is that really faulty religion, improper practice? I hear that all beliefs rely on those shelters; they appear to be little comfort houses and structures of consolation."

"Friend, daughter, they lead to accounting occasions of the spirit against pre-calibrated calendars, maps and charts. Spiritual events simply do not abide by the calendar. The birth of Jesus —all of the conformations of God —these were from all time, always; and not in Bethlehem alone, but all places, in every place we might pray in faith. Admittedly, they have been reinforced by special Presences during my lifetime. But remember that Bethlehem, for example, is everywhere and nowhere at all times and at no time, outside time. I am not certain I could say `everywhere, always —nowhere, never' if I had not stood there then."

"Yet, I find great personal happiness in the fact that you did accompany those events, Papa."

"But those occurrences simply impress on me the cleverness of mankind. People invented time to avoid admitting bewilderment over events."

"Would you not favor yearly celebrations, such as some have become? Should we not assemble for such festivals?"

"Yes, please invite them, daughter, but do not let people draw curtains around these spectacles. Let them be seen!"

"Curtains? Time curtains? Here-and-there stage and arena curtains?"

"You understand, Johara. Any of them should be celebrated any time the mind, the spirit, is disposed and readied. Incarnation, Passover, Crucifixion, Pentecost —these Godly constellations occur any day; no need to separate them. Be supple; celebrate them every day; give honor in your childlike joy; resist attempts to slice time with clocks and calendars. No one on the Way to becoming childlike is a mere wanderer."

Johara became solicitous; "Papa, many say that you possess a prophetic gift. I insist: Won't you please share your views on the future?"

"Well, I am also among those who trust in my gifts! That gift, that inspiration guided me in the Epistle we —your Mother and I —wrote a few years ago; you want more, right?" Johara nodded and touched his cheek in affirmation. "Let us call up a view of some 20 years ahead; I predict that people who thrive on calendar-making and shrine construction will commit many frauds in the year that will be marked as the 100th year of Jesus. They will prescribe the Second Coming; they will likely identify various articles of merchandise, various services that believers should purchase. Why? To ennoble their souls, sellers will claim. Yes. And I foresee events when the further passage of time will bring the world to the Year numbered One thousand."

"Or Two thousand, Papa!" cheered Johara.

"Yes," Silas agreed, "but the mystery of the millennium may tempt many in future generations to take the Devil's guidance, tempt them to prescribe tricks for Heaven and to set fees for salvation.

"Yes, oh yes, Johara," he observed, picking up a glossy stone that lay within reach. He looked intently at it as he continued, "I can hear them: First, they say, 'Purchase this globe of glass; in it you can view your seat in Heaven, when the Morning Star aligns with the Sun.' Later, 'Buy this key, take this key at dawn on the millennial year; it fits the lock that holds your heavenly treasure....' Those future merchants will have their fees from faith in material myths. But some of our descendants will hold fast to faith in spiritual myths, reliable myths reinforced by trust of believers. Those future children give me a view, a peek, at a picture of hope."

FEASTING WITH THE DEACON

"Yes, then tell me, Father, more details of the hopeful outcome you can envision; share it with me. It will strengthen my own heart for the climb I must still make." Johara moved closer to hear each word, since Silas spoke as in a reverie, as if translating a dream.

"In the ultimate," the deacon offered, "before the end of all things, God will subdue the Satanic evils by embracing them. As in the Beginning, Lucifer will add to the praises and intensify the light. There is no other outcome possible," Silas confided in a strong whisper to his daughter. "All evil will finally disappear in love, dissolved in God's Infinity."

"Papa, I think it is time to ponder my cooking," Johara said after a time of silence. When she had started her fires and prepared her stews, Johara let them stand warm and returned to the chair beside Silas' cot. She reached behind her head and scooped a small handful of raisins. She counted out to ten, aloud, and handed the dried grapes to her father. "Papa, can we continue this a little longer by taking a look at the Commandments —the Ten Commandments? For example, I have, at last, realized that men and women can disobey them. Every one of us can disobey all of the Commandments."

"Yes...? Or, we might otherwise all explode with praise."

"Papa, have some more raisins! Or make yourself welcome to those juicy figs; take them, but let me finish, please! What if everyone chose to separate from goodness by such failures?"

"Johara, you open an interesting question." He leaned his head into his open hands and was momentarily silent. As he began, he looked across the valley toward the great Thermaic Gulf as if he could see forever across the Aegean Sea. But he spoke in the quiet manner she had grown to know, and she could hear the perpetual boyishness that characterized her father's ways. Silas was the observer, and he reported his sightings, repeating her name: "Johara, our scholarly Greek friends in Athens and Alexandria would dispute your supposition on mathematical grounds. They would say you have attempted the impossible, the destruction of the number 2."

"How is that, Papa? I am talking about violation of any and all ten commandments by everyone. I do not follow the scholars, I guess."

Silas continued his musings, laying two small twigs across the end of the table where they sat. "They would say that two people, one man and one woman, left to survive, would assure that two of the commandments would not be broken by everyone. Otherwise, how could they commit murder?"

Johara struck brightly at the question: "Why, the wrong could occur easily within the mind of the survivor. Sins, as well as virtues reside in the mind, in the spirit, do they not, Papa?"

Silas cleared his throat to buy time, whose vendors slipped into the doorway, unseen by the deacon: Melana and Joshua had returned early from Edhessa; not seen by Johara or Silas, they —especially Melana —stood enjoying this loving quest for light on truths, insofar as that light could come to Berea. Still not seeing his wife and son, but sensing a measure of change in the air, Silas laughed and continued the discussion with Johara. "Your tongue and spirit do delight me, daughter. I repeat, you did open an interesting question," Silas said.

"You know, your concern seems well placed, but God does know what will actually happen."

"Yes?"

"Johara, I do not believe the Commandments were offered as a spiritual suicide pact. They assure happiness, and the Author counts on the appetite some people have for happiness, even if only a handful possess that appetite and mold praises."

"But —"

"Johara!" her mother called, catching them both by surprise. While they seemed to ask 'when did you return?' Melana continued, "Silas, I once heard you say that you came to Berea as if only you and God were starting work on the First Commandment. As long as one person intends to honor those Commandments, so glorifying God, God does not lose, I think. I also believe that the life of a person who glorifies can illustrate and actually magnify glorifications she voiced at an earlier time."

"Mother! That is truly beautiful!" Johara cheered, joined by her brother and Silas.

Having regained the stage for a bit, Johara urged, "All three of you get into some lovely songs while your youngest cook sets a meal. With songs, you can provide the setting for my spiritual exercises, you know —although Papa has stretched my understanding today."

So they sang and ate Johara's supper and sipped a warm drink made of young peach-leaf steepings, and they all skipped in the lantern light. Then they recited night prayers and went to bed.

FEASTING WITH THE DEACON

Berea kept watch, but slept. Miles to the west, Vesuvius spewed millions of tons of ash and molten earths out across the cities of Pompeii and Herculaneum. The eruptive disaster would put a call on the Deacon's house.

CHAPTER 18.

Year 80 A.D. —RECALLING A NOURISHER

"Let me then die and pray for the joyful repose of my soul."— Epistle of Silas/

Havens, Near Herculaneum
March, in the First Year of Titus the Emperor
Dear Mother, Father and Johara

I am writing from the shacks that we built last winter to house the refugees from Vesuvius. The Emperor, who was ungenerous to the Jerusalem exiles ten years ago, sent substantial funds and troops here to build new housing, roads and markets for those from Pompeii and nearby. Since we acknowledged that we will couple our charity with a hope to evangelize, we have been denied public funds to provide wards for injured, ill and recovering neighbors. I have learned how to raise monies in various ways —do not be concerned about their propriety! I am, first of all, your son and brother.

We have plenty of food, and much of it appears to come from gardens quite like ours in Berea. The Romans/Pompeiians eat both goat and pig meat and seem rather fond of sauces. Papa Geronis (I shall call you Geronis, since you have to accept that you are my oldest relative), Papa, you will be pleased to learn that I (with help) have mastered some of the secrets of these cooks. I shall try to show you my newest skills in sauces when I come home after this task is complete

This task I welcome. I find good works make it easier for me to describe the noble teachings we bring —such soul healing, spirit support, is easier for me than preaching or encouraging a free-running debate. I do not require any special reasoning to pick up the injured, bind their wounds and feed them. In turn, they often ask just the questions that let me confess that my work, my deeds, are but little mirrors of my desire, my burning in love for them.

You know, Johara, you are the one who has Father's zeal and homing sense for those who are both receptive and needy; that, plus the fact that you have the combined ability to debate, which Mother possesses. I think it is quite proper that I tell all three of you (by way of this letter being sent by a Christian bearer to Berea) that our family best shows me how to live and serve. I suppose some would have pushed me (the vigorous boy-child) into the wild mission fields; they would have urged Johara to perpetuate the sick-care and neighborly charity that Lydia accomplished so easily; many do so expect their daughters to adopt that form to practice homemaking, prior to marriage, I observe.

I want to say that I was not prepared at first for the spiritual destruction that came upon many of the survivors during the past Winter. One might have expected that if their wounds healed and their bones mended, only the need for enough good food to nourish our homeless would remain. That turned out to be misleading. Indeed, they do suffer anguish over their losses, some irrecoverable possessions, and friends or family now dead. However, a lot of care has been invested in shedding the sense of guilt by survivors. We and they will not easily dismiss the randomness and impersonal nature of earthquakes and volcanic action. They personalize the fact that they were spared and their old neighbors suffered for no apparent reason on either side of it.

Their spiritual state reminds me of the course of spiritual sickness that Caleb suffered, and yet, I still do not understand his problems. I can comprehend the love a man may confess for a woman married to another but also would have thought his own internal counsel would have told him to let it go, while loving Mother. Dare I ask you, Mother, how you handled it, and whether you have advice on similar situations that Johara and I may face? Of course, I do not understand it all, either, but I can show that I do not feel guilty about being alive here, just joyful in my work.

Oh yes, we do sing a lot, and I have taught several Greek hymns to those brought here. One of the refugees is a lovely red-haired maid named Timna who will likely take up an increasing share of my attention. I understand that her parents are immigrant Jews from settlements in Tarshish. With them, she studied the teaching of Paul when he preached the Way of the Master in those parts of Iberia some years ago. She has taught me a local skip dance from CaesarAugusta. Perhaps I can (make that we can!) illustrate for you some time.

I must finish this scroll and pack it with the pair of sandals Timna made for Mother, since the runner, the bearer, is to leave for Brundisium later this morning, heading across the Sea of Adria for Dyrrhachium and on to Berea (you called it the Ionian Sea, Papa).

I send love and wishes for your health and happiness. Please write; I shall be here at the havens, God willing, until mid-summer.

Your son and brother,

Joshua.

Added note: I don't know how I could have forgotten it, when I mentioned the "help" I have had in learning ways to cook: There are two outstandingly skilled cooks who have come to help, and they both recall you!!

One of the cooks is a woman from Hibernia, the Celtic isles of Britannia. She is a beautiful person called FionaFair; she helps everyone and knows how to transform simple leaves and buds or stems, seeds and nuts into tasty recipes.... That's not all: A woman named Tamara is with her; Tamara recalls both Papa and our pathetic neighbor, Caleb, especially from experiences at Dyrrachium. She says her life now is 'on course to joy' as a result of counsel from you and Titus and her friendship with Fiona. Of course, Tamara is no longer young, and she has lost most of her teeth, but she still has an air that shows how proudly and beautifully she once carried herself. She told me that she has re-built her life as a result of Papa's directions toward 'holy intervention.' Lovely....

"Dosh

FINAL FEAST WITH THE DEACON

The Springhouse, Berea, June, in the First Year of the Reign of Titus Vespasianus

My dearest Johara,

Your father has been lying on his cot looking out at Vermion's slope. I have only now finished reading Joshua's letter aloud to him; then he (the older man with blue eyes, such that God made no matches to them) —your Papa insisted he would read it silently to himself! Joking, he said Josh exceeds the bounds of respect by calling him Geronis. "What does he mean?

What 'old man' does Joshua address here?" Papa asked. Me? Surely not!" Then he chuckled and hummed one of Joshua's favorite songs.

You will find Joshua's letter enclosed here, of course. I told Papa I would immediately start a letter to you; the Berean youths who volunteered to bring you supplies stopped by to say they will be leaving at dawn to carry two baskets of goods into the Galatian hill country where you are. Papa and two others who worship with us made the little wooden crosses that I have wrapped for you to give to newcomers to the faith as you distribute joy and love.

We also got up this morning to make the cakes that you will find in the yellow basket. Your Papa is almost too weak to organize the ingredients and get them into the oven, but we succeeded today. Another success of the day has been the completion of the Epistle your father began some time before he came to Berea. He made notations and prayerful commentary during the past 20 years, and I am greatly complimented to realize that he and I collaborated on it to construct its ending. I find it very well done, and have made it a part of his combined works. You and Joshua will want to borrow from it and share it with the entire community. I have set aside the complete scroll, but have not included it with the food and wine and other supplies being sent to you.

The jugged red wine is from the festival earlier this month, very good. Just a small glass exercises our bellies to a proper liveliness. Speaking of the virtues of wine reminds me of both Paul and Caleb, now passed to another eternity. Paul became a model for many, although his sanctity was exaggerated by both himself and some of his close followers. We do need more who pattern their minds after his....

On Caleb, the Rebel who died long before his heart stopped, I will say that he often tried to treat me as his own property —a conveyance of goods that no woman should permit, and I did not.

After your father and I married, we concluded that Caleb would be our prayer target, and we simply ignored his lust. I prayerfully acknowledged that Caleb carried an infestation of Caleb-ness in his make-up and that I did not understand his make-up. It appears that he never came to understand 'Melana-ness', either —as if I completely understand myself! Praise the Holy Names and feast on their gifts....

Do you have a recipe for the cakes we are sending? Papa wanted you to have it; it is easy to memorize, for anyone who lived in this home. We have always called it 'Silas's Seduction', but it really does not threaten anyone's virtue!

First, make a syrup of honey, water, cloves, citrus peel and white wine; use your good sense to decide the amounts, but do make it subtly spicy.

Heat the syrup-mix and set it aside to cool a bit before you add the wine;

The mix will provide a topping for the cake.

The cake combines sweet crumbs with four times their volume in crushed nuts, especially crushed almonds.

Add egg yolks and honey, about equal parts, using separated yolks from about eight eggs for two measured cups of sweet crumbs.

When you have a smooth blend of this mix, add frothed egg whites from the same eight eggs.

Add this batter mixture gently into a pan you have oiled with lamb's fat. Then bake your cake for an hour in an oven hot enough to make a drop of water dance and vanish in about a blink of the eye.

When the cake has cooled from the oven, add the spiced honey topping and eat. Eat, but with caution!

Papa Silas says it is so good it will always require speedy destruction! You children always begged for it, but we could not get almonds for the past 12 years or so; now the shops here are full of them. Let us know if you need a supply there.

I must get this scroll folded and placed into the basket, so will end it quickly with our love and best wishes. By the way, both of us smiled over the use of "holy intervention," as Josh reports some people call your father's form of ministry. I like that, and wish that I had so correctly named it.

With love, as ever,
Mother (and Papa Silas!)

EPISTLE OF SILAS benGaddiel TO THE MISSIONS
(found as a codex with manuscript of "**Feasting with the Deacon**")...BELOVED:

I, Silas, Servant at Berea, pray for and await the continued guidance of the Spirit.

Having worked with our departed friends, Saul and Cephas, and having witnessed our increase in numbers here in Macedonia, I hope I reflect that guidance to the Way in this letter to you, sisters and brothers afar, and in times yet to come.

The Trinity will lead us all to answers on diverse matters. Be vigilant. Take heed of our message, which we present here in sets of Truth, in **Emets**.

Greetings, Brothers and Sisters, in the Names of God-our-Lord.

Emet I.

I speak to you of prayer and praise. Set your souls warmly aglow with prayer, that they may shine as lanterns on the mountainside, vanishing the darkness.

God in the Holy Spirit sets our souls afire when we pray, and He prizes our lamps when we glorify and praise Him. We may also beacon to others when we surrender and ask for blessings; therefore, open yourselves to receive them.

Yes, Pray, but keep in mind that God is not a servant. Providence, even in Its mysterious Almighty, does not reverse time or invert space, nor yet cancel the forces set to run between the earth, the clouds and the sun.

Confine your attention to prayerful concerns about health, happiness and your love for others. In praying, watch for new ways to add glories to God's holy Names.

Praying within the embrace of the Compassionate Redeemer, we better our aims and walk the path to more pure and complete happiness; observe, dear cousins and loved friends —prayers that join many minds multiply their blessings. You must not claim that events which parallel your prayers are new miracles, but you may correctly honor old miracles, such as life. May we will to follow the guidance we request. Hallelujah!

Emet II.

When you pray together, you receive blessings that exceed your hopes. Yes, you may gather many in common prayer, but God grants no evil ends, and the death of an enemy should not be credited as an answer to prayer. The Everlasting extends more lots of spiritual prizes than are drawn —treasures surpassing all desires or merits. We cannot merit the spiritual treasures given, whether we ask for the gifts for ourselves or for others, yes, even if we do not ask for them. This is all a great mystery. Some parts of the mystery were opened to me, and I shall tell you those disclosures —all which words will allow. Each person at prayer increases the power in the prayers of all like minds, enlarging and multiplying the forces of the Spirit. However, Love and the other forces of the Spirit do not exist alone, in solitude; they gather sinews and strength from the number sharing them. For Love itself requires an object, namely, that which is to be loved. Here, I speak beyond the wonder of fires and fuels, drawing on the secret of Alpha —of beginnings, that God may be praised by all of creation.

Emet III.

Do not doubt this: praying glory to God is the most noble and cherished act we can perform. God created us to share in His glory and, by praise, to send Him glory and to anticipate the happiness of Paradise. In proper accord with that purpose, find your present happiness and increase your future feasting by lifting up songs and praise to the Lord —our Three-Person God. Many in Berea and over in Thessalonica have asked whether our spiritual treasures add to the fullness of God, and I must tell you this question will remain worrisome until the darkness ends.

Yet, even in our dim understanding, we see that souls do fall short and lament; they long for communion with the Perfection cut off through their unbelief and wrongdoing.   God, who is perfect indeed, cannot suffer from any wound we intend to impose on Him, even in reasonable anger. He will overcome all wrongful intention; by the end of time, God's love shall transform Satan, evil becoming love.

Does God, then, suffer any need? Yes, God needs to reward us for needing Him in the perfect presence. Let us work in accord with that need, glorifying God in the light, by which we most nearly approach perfection. When we send songs of praise to God, we reflect the purpose of our lives, ennobling our souls, but I have no special wisdom on this matter. Clearly, we should not strain on trifles or choke on fine-choppings of the law when we offer God praises.

If we only intend to glorify Him, God is thereby glorified, adding to the Infinite.

The GodHead expands in our praise but derives no benefit from sacrifices. However, we do not diminish It if we cease giving glory; we may thereby foster our own darkness. This is Aletheia, **Emet**, Truth; but altogether, it is a great Mystery.

Emet IV.

You suffer another puzzlement: You have asked about encounters in Paradise. How will you recognize children who have grown tall after your deaths, or will you know friends who have become wrinkled long after separations here? I reply that you will want nothing in a new and perfect entirety of yourselves, whole in mind and spirit. You will be above discriminations of the flesh in that perfection.

When I was speaking at Thessalonica, a man inquired, "How will my sister in Heaven know me? I have already grown bald and full of warts and scars since she died?" I was correct in the Lord, when I answered, "Neither brother or sister will want, not for any thing. You will not then embrace or shun baldness, warts, circumcisions, wombs or the lack of such attributes." Matters more noble than these should command our attention, but these are appealing. I accept that God's love will envelop our admission of confusion over little absurdities.

Better to try to work through such puzzles as might a child than that the soul despair over emptiness.

Anticipate that the Way will bring us the bliss of perfect fullness! In our incomplete illumination, we praise Creator, Son and Spirit, forever One. Hunger for new ways to give praise; find them; follow them. Pray and praise.

Emet V.

Believe this: Happiness comes from giving glory because it suits God's best purpose to receive our praise, and it is in our happiness that we realize our fullness of being.

Glorify God in your closet or as you stand in the open field or as you walk the dry desert alone.

Glorify God when you suffer deepest loss, or when abandoned, or when thieves have taken your goods.

FEASTING WITH THE DEACON

In extreme joy or deepest despair, glorify God to bring close His comforting presence and gifts.

Stifle your cries for provisions for your needs; God already knows our needs before they fall on us; our proper task is to praise the Names of God. Our needs vanish in the prosperity of spirit and the richness of life that follows.

Again, I say this is Aletheia, Emet, the Truth: that we should show our appetite for new ways to give praise.

Find songs at dawn in Winter, when the sun halos the mountain tops endowed with snow; show gladness.. On the Sabbath or on other days that may be set aside, take a place apart with a few friends, praising the Master's Name for all blessings; or take a place with a multitude who celebrate mysteries in a temple adorned with jewels.

Immerse yourselves in the Way of Truth; know the Word and romp in It as a child at play.

Do not become tangled in the law; if you stumble, you may still receive redemption. Emet, the Truth.

Share love and give glory Amen.

Emet VI.

Pray that you may come to know death, even as Jesus, who is the Truth, knew death. On a pillow of radiance and childlike love, we may let this life slip away.

Preserve life and keep its gifts as long as they bring you the prospect of happiness and the means of glorifying God.

When the body is no longer a place for the soul to prosper and praise, let the flesh die; God did it no harm. No, God cannot do harm, and harms not even those who despise Him; for Truth and Love walk as companions in virtue, steadying and sheltering the soul, but authoring no hurt.

Shun harmdoing; pray for those who render harm; otherwise, how will Love win Satan, as It shall in the end?

Many wounds can befall my body, yet it still provides a residence for my soul; bring praises!

Consider, we are all mortal, and my body will come to a condition from which it shall not then recover; yours, likewise. Oils and balms then applied will not restore strength or voice; let me then die.

Pray, then for the joyful repose of my soul; my soul, uttering the Holy Names, may return to the Author of its nobility. Now, in confident assurance that I shall see you again, and with special greetings from Melana, from our children and from the entire church at Berea, I hold you in my prayers, joined by all who approach a new childhood with me.

AMEN...

*\SILAS benGaddiel, the Deacon at Macedonian Berea,
In the Third Year of Vespasian's rule/*

CHAPTER 19.

A NOURISHER CALLED HOME

"God already knows our needs before they fall on us; our proper task is to praise the names of God."/ Epistle of Silas

***

Berea
July 13
in the First Year of the Reign of the Emperor Titus
Johara, My dear Sister:

Papa just died, and it was as if he had simply gone to sleep again. Only last night, Timna and I returned from Herculaneum and joined him with a glass of wine, a bowl of figs and the joy of a last song with him. Timna has had a lot of experience with the first song becoming the last, she remarked. Mother seemed to know, in those hours just before he left us for the other life. She made two memorable comments: One, that he declared that he should 'on the morrow', prepare to give glory more lovingly, and two, that he asked to hold the seashell Peter gave him in Rome. He was listening to the seashell at the end.

The courier who last saw you said he will assure that you hurry home. We will proceed to bury Papa up by the springs whose refreshing waters he so loved. Please remember his last prayer, which was among the first he learned as a boy in the Valley of the Jordan. It began: *'Baruch atah adonai eloha-inu melech ha-olan.'*. Beautiful, even in the Hebrew we do not understand! In our tongue: **'Blessed are You, Lord our God, King of the Universe....'** Of course, we will have summer flowers for his grave. Mother and I and Timna will mark it for you and for those of future times who will admire and follow the ways he taught, since they copy the Way of The Master.

\"Pray, then, for the joyful repose of my soul."/ Epistle of Silas...

LEONARD BARRY BARRINGTON

In brotherly love,
Joshua.

***

Berea, August, in the Third Year of the Reign of Titus
Dear Joshua,
Your little sister doesn't write letters very often, does she? Well, here is one, accompanying the herbs and spices you asked for in your last note. I am quite certain that you know, better than I, how sparingly they should be added to stews and sweets to call out their best spirits.

Since I have started a letter, I will add a few thoughts and bits of news. For news, I should tell you that I have decided to localize my mission work and to minister around here. Perhaps those who incline to my teachings will go beyond the territory, as I have briefly, but I want to blanket these marvelous Macedonians with love, as Mother and Papa did.

I look up the path that begins in the low thickets near Berea's well, to the place where Papa lies buried. The grass there has turned brittle dry this year. I went with Mother up there last week and felt strongly lifted in her presence along that loft of hill where the cedar tree bends —just as Mother, without apparent tiring, faced that unending wind....

Mother has grown white-haired during the past months, but she is still Papa's brown beauty. She was so lovely kneeling in the diminished sunlight there, where we visited his grave, prayed and sang. I realize that the words may weigh a bit heavily in a letter, but she chanted it so prettily:

> **Thank you for the gardens he planted,**
> **The plants he watered,   The children he fathered,**
> **The prayers and sermons he uttered,**
> **The help he gave the homeless,**
> **And the days and nights he loved me.**
> `I come praising your Holy Names for the peace
> which he tried to forge in his anger over injustice, keeping him
> true.

There, see! No dirges, just joy drums, dear Brother. Thus, your journey and mine extend along the Way, following the course Papa and Mother and their companions began; the journey, it seems to me, will never end, but goes beyond, beyond to banquets that glorify it. Mine is to be here; and we in Berea, Edhessa, and Thessalonica will need help, much as you will require assistance on the road from Pompeii/ Herculaneum to Rome.

Please write. If you know anyone who wishes to nurture with spiritual food and who has much love to share, tell them to come over into Macedonia. I look for the day when I may book a ship to the port of Rome, and ask you and the fair-browed Timna to escort this 'young one' on a tour of THE City. I am so pleased that she married you. Papa would have hugged her and chatted with her in a double-hang-on-every-word conversation. I strongly suspect that he's invading the talk between the two of you even now; don't be jealous!!

Mother is likely to read my letter before it's dispatched to you. Johara.

Post Script from Mother Melana to Timna and Dosh —I did read it, and I agree: Silas, your Father, would have enjoyed long chats with Timna, and we would have had *such* a time. However, I do not want to call him back ——not even for all that rollicking conversation, laughter and dancing in the kitchen. As well as dreams.... We do have recipes for happy dreams ——right? Mother Melana

FLORAL BRIEF

When we observe the flowers that bloom blossoming in early Spring, (The velvet-lobate primrose and the nobly petaled roses), We also hear their spirits sing And note the Truth which good-and-pure discloses.
END OF "FEASTING WITH THE DEACON"/
Leonard F. Barry Barrington 1998-2006